THE SUFFERING

DAN MAYER

ISBN: 978-1-61296-962-6
PUBLISHED BY BLACK ROSE WRITING
www.blackrosewriting.com

Printed in the United States of America
Suggested Retail Price (SRP) $17.95

The Suffering is printed in Adobe Garamond Pro

To Patricia, a constant source of support and inspiration. To Krista, who showed me, didn't tell me, and to Cora, my Mom and Louanne, who read it first.

THE
SUFFERING

PROLOGUE

Can you truly be sure if it's your time to die? We have all felt miserable, many times in our lives. Many of us have uttered the words, "I feel like I'm going to die." But, do we ever truly know when it's our time? I guess we might know for sure if we were in a horrific accident, had been shot, or if we were diagnosed with a terminal illness. Would we then know, we were going to die, or would we still hold on to the hope of life? Does your life really, flash before your eyes, as they say? Do you have more regrets than you have accomplishments? Are you pleased with your life, or are you sorry for the suffering that you have caused?

CHAPTER ONE

The air became colder as dusk approached. The birds slowed their ceaseless chatter and the squirrels tucked themselves away for the night. Seconds crawled into minutes and minutes into hours. With each passing second, he was happy to be alive, yet with each passing minute he wondered, how time could possibly pass, so slowly by.

The weatherman had forecasted snow in the higher elevations. He was about half way up the mountain and snow seemed likely. A strange stillness overtook the forest; as if nature held her breath, waiting for him to die, but he wouldn't go easily. Not without a fight.

He could see his breath rising above his lips and spreading in a plume of condensation, before dissipating into the now colder air. He knew that if he didn't do something, that death would be inevitable. Not some time far in the future when he was old and grey, but soon, all too soon. He could tell when it happened, that his right leg was broken, he didn't need a doctor for that. He was in for one hell of a long night, if he made it that long.

He could smell the strong, pungent scent of evergreen, dead leaves and earth. Water trickled from the rock face nearby, gathering in a small pool below. Dried blood covered his face and plugged his right nostril. He could feel the warmth of his blood soaking his hair and shirt, and the searing pain, in what was left of his right hand.

If he believed in God, he would be praying; to be saved, to live, but not for salvation. He knew that it was far too late for that. He also knew that he missed his brother something fierce. Henry had been gone for three years now.

The light faded faster now. The sun seemed to race to get over the horizon, to get out of sight, so that darkness could fill the world again. The thought of spending all night in the dark was almost too much to bear. He had always been afraid of it.

He summoned as much energy as he could and called out: "Help! Help me!"

No one heard his cries. He slumped back into the leaves and the dirt, exhausted. He wheezed with every painful draw of breath and every exhale produced a raspy, phlegmy noise that he couldn't cough to clear.

A coyote began to howl at the moon. Its lonely cry, echoed off the mountain and got caught in the trees far below. It was followed by another and then another, getting closer. They could probably smell the blood and the fear, the inevitability of death.

An owl landed on a branch in front of him and asked him: "Who? Who?" That was as good a question as there was, but he didn't have an answer for him. He certainly wasn't the person that he started out to be. Time and circumstances had seen to that. The owl sat for a while looking at him, waiting, before it flew off to find someone else to talk to.

He had to get busy and find some way to keep himself warm, or he was going to die of hypothermia. That was if the blood loss, didn't get him first.

The surrounding leaves would have to serve as a make-shift blanket. He used his left hand to pull them from the area to cover himself. Almost immediately he began to feel warmer, which buoyed his spirits a little. If he could make it until morning; he was sure that some hiker would find him, and he would be saved.

The darkness pressed down upon him and he closed his eyes to escape from it. He awoke several hours later. The blanket of stars now overhead, illuminated the mountain ever so slightly. It was enough to keep the fear of the dark at bay. He tried to re-position himself but his battered body protested and made moving very difficult. It was as though he was buried in sand. At least he was still alive.

There was a rustling in the leaves to his right and his heart rate accelerated. He was scared that it was a coyote coming to finish him off. The extra blood flow made his hand scream with pain and he held it gingerly in the air, to stop the throbbing. He turned his head slowly to meet his attacker, but it was nothing more than a couple of raccoons, rustling about in the leaves looking for something to eat. They seemed uninterested by his presence and continued on their way. He watched them until they were out of sight and went back to staring at the stars. He could never remember a time, when the stars looked so plentiful, so bright. Instead of soothing him, it made him feel smaller, more desperate. He was like a speck of sand on a beach.

There was a lot of woods on this mountain to explore. It would take a bit of luck for someone to find him, soon enough to save him. The only thing going for him, was that a stranger wouldn't know him. They might leave him to die, if they knew what he was capable of, what he had done.

The pain in his hand diminished and so he lowered his arm to his side. He had no idea what time it was. His watch had been smashed and rendered useless by the fall and he'd thrown it down the mountain in anger. He'd tried to crawl back to the hiking trail but he was unable to make it. Now it would be an impossible task.

He wished that he could clear his mind, if only for a little while, but that was always the problem. He was always thinking, always going over things in his head. A ceaseless barrage of thoughts, questions, images and sounds. He'd been here before. There were times in the past, he wished so badly that it would stop, wished that he would die, or better yet, that he had never been born. The world could get on just fine without him. Then someone would come along and they would make him feel better, they would 'fill him up'. Now that he was lying here on the precipice of death; it would be easy to let go and succumb to his injuries and welcome death, but now that he was this close, he found that he didn't want to die.

Clouds were starting to hide the stars overhead; slowly at first, but steadily increasing, until only a few could be seen peeking through the cloud cover. The first snowflake drifted lazily down and landed on the bridge of his nose. It melted but was replaced by another and then another, until they came so quickly that they accumulated on his skin, faster than they could melt. His head hurt too much to shake the snow from his face, and where it had melted it began to itch. He had no way to scratch it or remove the snow, and so he just lay there and tried to occupy his thoughts with something else. He couldn't. The itch was maddening and he had to scratch it and clear his face. He slowly and carefully positioned his left arm, where he could swipe at the snow. The relief was amazing, it actually made him smile, it felt so good. He left his arm in that position so that his hand was at the ready, when he needed to clear the snow once again.

The snow continued to fall and eventually his blanket of leaves was now a blanket of snow as well. When it had finished falling, he tucked his arm back under the leaves.

The clouds remained and the darkness of the night settled in around him again. He saw things lurking in the shadows. He heard things whispering in the night, unimaginable things. Things plotting and conspiring against him, things without any compassion or soul. He saw people he once knew with them, hiding, peering out from behind trees and rocks, ready to exact their revenge, to receive their payment in blood, ready to end his miserable life.

"Go on, do your worst," he whispered to the darkness.

No one replied. They were biding their time, waiting for the right moment, waiting until he was at his most vulnerable.

He wished that the owl would return to talk to him. He wasn't sure what he would say to him, if he did.

He began to smell something through his unplugged nostril. At first, he imagined that it was cigarette smoke. There was someone close by. He was saved. He nearly cried out to the darkness, pleading for help. Then he realized that it was the scent of wood burning in a woodstove, in some cabin far below. People were tucked warmly in their beds, sleeping, dreaming pleasant dreams and getting ready for the new day ahead, unaware of his life and death struggle, nearby.

He could almost smell fresh brewed coffee, filling the small cabin, bacon and eggs frying on the stove and bread toasting in the toaster. His mouth began to water slightly as he thought of breakfast being prepared. His stomach rumbled. He hadn't eaten anything since lunch. His back pack was lost when he tumbled down to where he lay, battered, bruised, and bleeding, but alive.

He pulled some snow into his hand and brought it to his mouth. The soothing cold was heaven to his lips and parched throat. It certainly wasn't breakfast but it was wonderful nonetheless. The dry, burning, was relieved for the time being.

It seemed lighter now, but it might be just wishful thinking, after a long and mostly sleepless night.

No, he could see further into the forest now than he had been able to, only moments before. He might make it after all.

A thought pried into his mind but he pushed it away. He wanted a moment of happiness. It persisted, wanted to be heard. He tried to enjoy the retreat of the darkness. The light gathered itself and made one final push to start the day. The sun rose above the trees and a sliver of orange peeked over the horizon.

That persistent thought finally broke through when he was pre-occupied with the sunrise. It was Monday. It wasn't the weekend when most hikers and weekend warriors took to the mountain for their weekly exercise. It was Monday. People rarely came to the mountain on Monday. Some people that worked shift work would come, that's true, but that was a small percentage of the hikers. It was mostly office workers, suburbanites and yuppies, getting in touch with nature, who made the trek up the mountain.

He didn't like his odds of being found. He didn't like them one little bit. There were fifteen different trails that criss-crossed the mountain.

Even the sun that was now sitting above the tree tops couldn't buoy his spirits. He closed his eyes and wept.

CHAPTER TWO

William Pope Johnson was born in Galway Ireland in 1940. His father was a carpenter and someday he would follow in his Dad's footsteps.

Every Sunday they would all make the walk across town, down by the river Corrib and through the narrow cobblestone streets, to go to Mass. He held his Father's hand as they made their way through the crowded streets. Everyone was decked out in their Sunday best and he was proud to wear his nice new suit. His Father didn't make a lot of money and he knew how special it was to have such a fine suit. He was the youngest of five siblings and the only boy. His sisters were all older than he was and they ranged in age from twelve to eighteen, he had just turned eight.

His Mother died giving birth to him. He had seen many pictures of her and his Dad told him all about her, any time that he asked.

"I don't mind, son. Talking about her makes me feel closer to her; besides she's my favourite topic in all the world. She looked a lot like you, you know? But then, you've heard me say that many times before. Let's see if I can't think of a story that you haven't heard. I know. Have I ever told you about the day I taught her to fish?"

"No, haven't heard that one."

"It was a nice summer day and we took a little row boat onto the pond on her cousin's property. We were trying to catch perch. I thought it was a good idea to start her off small. I tied her hook and then put a minnow on it. No different than when I first started taking you fishing, when you were a wee lad. I showed her how to use the reel and how to set the hook and it wasn't a minute before she got a bite. She was a natural. She set the hook and her pole bent right down to the water, but it wasn't moving. I told her that she must have snagged the bottom and showed her how to try and jerk it free. A couple of tugs and that mean old pike on the other end, had had about enough of that, and he took off for the other side of the pond and brought the boat with him. He dragged us all over that pond, until he tired enough for us to land him. It was one of the craziest things that I had ever seen, that fish dragging us around like that. It was the biggest darned pike that I ever set me eyes on, in my whole life. I swear to God. To this very day, I've never seen one bigger. Your Mom was so proud of that fish. She wanted to go fishing all the time after that. You know what I remember most about that day? It wasn't the warmth of the day or even the fish that she caught. It was the smile on your Mom's face. When I saw her sweet smile; I knew that she was the one, that I wanted to spend the rest of my life with," he said, wiping tears from the corners of his eyes.

"Are you okay, Dad?"

"I'm fine son. I cry sometimes when I think of your Mom. There's no shame in crying. There are sad tears and there are tears of joy, and sometimes there are both; like when I think of your Mom. She was a beautiful person; inside and out. I only hope that, through these stories that I tell you, I can somehow find the words to describe, how wonderful she was."

Bill could hear the love in his Dad's voice, see it in his eyes, and he did feel closer to his Mom, with every new story that he told.

His Dad did his best caring for him and his sisters, but there wasn't a lot of money to go around. He worked hard to provide for his family and he worked long hours and sometimes Saturdays as well. Sundays were always special, because they never missed Sunday Mass. They went as a family, spent the day and then had Sunday dinner together. Sunday was for God and family he said.

"Everything that we have, we owe to God. You are all gifts from God; your Mom included, and we have to trust that he had a purpose when He took her from us. God's will, is not to be questioned. We must trust that He knows what's best," he said, while we sat down for Sunday dinner.

Bill didn't understand at the time; he was too young. He would understand later, when he got older.

Every Sunday they went to Bohermore cemetery where their Mother was laid to rest. Many times, their Dad would tell stories about his Father and about their Mother, while they visited their gravesites. His sisters would also have stories to tell about Mom and Grandad. Bill was a little jealous that they got to know them, and that he never did. He sometimes felt like he was a bit of an outsider in the family because of it.

Bill was named after his Father and his Grandfather. His Grandfather's name was Conor Johnson and so he was named William Pope Conor Johnson.

He was always called Bill from the time he was born until the day he died. His Father always went by William, however. Bill found that fitting. He could never see his Father being called Bill. Bill wasn't a proud name like William was.

His Dad never took another wife and he spent as much of his spare time with his family as he could.

Occasionally he would stop at the pub for a pint, but that was about the extent of his time away from the family. It was on one of these brief stops that Bill got to experience first hand, just how great of a man his Father was. He never boasted or called attention to himself, but everyone that knew him, looked up to him.

They went to Murphy's pub down by the river, after work one day. His Dad ordered a pint of Guinness and he just had a glass of water. Several people made a point of shaking his Dad's hand as they entered or left. He wasn't a regular at the pub. They knew him from his quality workmanship and his calm, friendly demeanor. He was an honest man and he never spoke badly about another living soul.

The conversation they had was short and matter of fact, but it created a lasting impression. William got the barman to take a pint over to a man sitting by himself in the corner of the pub.

"Who's that guy? Is he a friend of yours?" Bill asked.

"That's someone that I've known for a very long time."

"Who is he?" Bill pressed.

"When I was a lad, I had a hard time fitting in. I got teased a bit in school. That man, was one of the boys that used to pick on me. He stole my lunch sometimes and he beat me up a couple of times."

"So, why in the world, would you ever buy him a drink?" Bill asked.

"Sometimes you have to look beyond people's actions. It wasn't me that he was angry with. He was unhappy with his lot in life. I've been blessed in my life; him not so much. I have wonderful children and before that I had a beautiful wife and loving parents. It's the very least that I can do, to buy that man a pint. It's my duty as a Christian and I take that very seriously," he said, and then sat

14

sipping his beer.

Just that; that simple statement, spoke volumes as to what kind of a man his Father was. He thought nothing of it and yet Bill was profoundly affected by it.

One by one his sisters got married and left the house, until it was just him and his Dad. They became even closer since it was only the two of them. Bill started to work as his Dad's apprentice. He enjoyed seeing how much people liked what they had created with their own hands, but most of all, he liked working with his Dad.

People would see him on the street and say things like, "Aren't you William Johnson's boy? He's as good as they come. You're one lucky lad, to have a Father such as him. Honest through and through, a good sausage that one. Hard-workin' fellow," they would say, and Bill would beam with pride, that they were speaking so highly of his Dad.

When he was sixteen, two- weeks shy of his seventeenth birthday, he went to work alone. His Dad wasn't feeling well and they had a job to finish by day's end. He had never gone to work without his Dad before, but he assured him that he was more than capable of doing the job. He insisted, that he was actually, better at his craft than he was. Bill didn't believe him, but he was proud as could be, that he would even consider him to be his equal.

He left in such high spirits that he whistled and sang all the way to work. It felt strange to be walking without his Dad, but he was going to make him proud, finish the job, and do it right.

He put in a long, hard day but at the end of it, he had accomplished what he had set out to do. The client was extremely happy with his work and he couldn't wait to get home to tell his Dad. He knew that he would be so proud of him.

He hurried home, flung open the door.

"I'm home!" he called out, but there was no answer.

He took off his shoes and went into the living room, he wasn't there. He wasn't feeling great when he left, so he thought maybe he went to lie down. He looked for him in his bedroom and sure enough he was in bed, having a nap. He could hardly wait to share his day with him, but he decided that it could wait until after he woke up. He cleaned up and made a delicious supper of fried chicken, green beans and fried potatoes and then went to wake him.

He walked slowly into his bedroom and knocked lightly on the door, so that he wouldn't startle him. He never stirred, so he walked around to the other side of the bed. He was lying on his side facing away from him. He walked up beside him and reached out his hand to shake him slightly and as he did, he got a terrible sick feeling. He knew before his hand ever landed on his Dad's shoulder. Deep down he knew, but he couldn't steel himself against the reality of the situation. He put his hand on his shoulder and shook him slightly. His Dad moved in an unnatural way. He was too rigid, too cold. He shook him harder hoping beyond hope, to wake him from a deep sleep. His Dad lay motionless in his bed. Bill threw himself on him and hugged him for all he was worth, trying to will him back to life. Tears ran down his face. He wept uncontrollably, in great retching, heartbreaking sobs. The blankets that covered his Dad's shoulder were soaked with tears when he was finally able to pull himself together. He slid a chair up close to his Dad's bed and reached out and held his hand for quite some time. He prayed for his Dad, himself and his sisters. He knew that they were going to be a mess when they found out as well, but they didn't share the same bond that he and his Dad did. His whole world had just changed in the blink of an eye. A moment ago, he was still a child and now he was an adult with all the worry and responsibility that that brought along with it.

He had to call his sisters and tell them the bad news, but he wasn't ready for that yet. He still needed some time alone with his Dad. He missed him already and he had only been gone a short time. He put his head down on the bed and cried and cried. He felt as though he might die as well. His eyes were all red and swollen and his throat felt like it was too small to swallow. His chest ached, he felt sick to his stomach and he was sweating profusely.

He couldn't imagine a world without his Dad in it, living the rest of his life without him. He was his hero. He was everything to him. They say that time heals everything, but he couldn't imagine that any amount of time would change how he felt at that moment.

"I love you Dad. I miss you already," he said, as he got up slowly.

He stood there looking at him for a long time, before reaching out and rubbing him on the shoulder.

"Please God give me the strength to carry on," he said, and then went into the kitchen to call his sister.

He called his eldest sister Abigail. She was the natural choice. She was also the most responsible one of the family, and was used to being in charge, when Dad wasn't home.

He had no idea what he was going to say. He didn't know if he could utter the words, Dad's dead. It seemed so final, like if he didn't admit it, then maybe he could somehow still change it. He went back to the doorway of his Dad's bedroom and looked in on him. He was still lying on his side facing away from him, the same way that he had left him.

He wiped the tears from his eyes and cleared his throat loudly. He walked to the kitchen sink and ran water from the faucet until it was cold. He splashed the water on his swollen eyes. He filled his hands, drank a couple of gulps of it, then turned off the tap and towelled himself dry.

He picked the phone from its receiver and dialled Abigail's number slowly. He didn't call her very often and when he did, it was because Dad had urged him to do so. He liked all his sisters just fine, but Abigail loved to talk and he didn't like talking on the phone all that much. He knew that Abigail would take care of everything, from this point on, and that's what he needed. He was too much of a mess to be of any help, to anyone right now.

"Hello?" he said cautiously.

"Well, hello Bill. How are you doin'? Haven't heard from you in a long time. It's funny you called, because we were just talking about you. I was just saying that we need to all get together for supper one night on the weekend. It's been a while since we were all under one roof."

It was at this point that Bill would usually hold the receiver away from his ear as she droned on, but he listened to every word.

"We need to start spending some more time together as a family you know. Dad's not going to be around forever and we, and by we, I mean the rest of the girls need to make a better effort to see Dad more often. You too sweetheart. I hope you didn't take that the wrong way, of course we want to see you too. Like I said, someday Dad will be gone and we need to still be a family, and if anything were to happen to Dad in the meantime, we would feel awful, just awful that we hadn't visited more. You know?" she continued, as Bill played with the phone cord.

"It's just that everyone gets caught up in work and driving the kids here, there and everywhere. A day goes by and then two and then a week and then two weeks and before you know it a couple of months go by. Oh, sure we still talk to Dad on the phone as often as we can, but we really need to make a better effort to come and see him and you face to face. Listen to me blabbering on. I'm sorry honey. What's up?" she said cheerfully, finally pausing to breathe.

When she did give him the chance to speak, he was at a loss for words. Bill didn't say anything. He just broke down and started to cry.

"Bill? Are you okay? What's happened? What's wrong? You can tell me, that's what big sisters are for," she said, and then her tone changed.

"Is Dad alright? Has something happened?" she asked.

He could hear the fear in her voice.

Bill cleared his throat and managed to croak out the words: "Dad's dead."

He heard the phone on the other end of the line strike the counter, as it fell to the floor.

"I'm on my way...I love you Bill," she said, when she came back on the line.

"Love you too," Bill said and hung up the phone.

He went and sat down at the kitchen table and waited for his sisters to arrive. Memories of his Dad flooded through his mind. He missed him so much already, it hurt. He began to cry again, something he did a lot of, in the next few days.

The next week was a blur. Abigail, and to a lesser extent his other sisters, helped with all the funeral arrangements, the internment and wake, which was a good thing because he was in no shape to help at all. He felt guilty that he couldn't talk at his Dad's funeral. He wrote a speech, but Abigail had to deliver it, because he couldn't get two words out without breaking into tears.

Abigail read, "My best friend in the entire world is gone. The world is not the same place as it was a few short days ago. The joy is gone and the world seems more grey to me. I want to talk about my hero. All of you here don't need to be told what kind of man my Father was. He was a proud man but not arrogant. He was a hard worker, but always made time for his family and God. He could be funny at times and he was always honest, always giving of his time. He was my teacher, my mentor, my hero, my friend and I miss him so much it hurts. They say that time heals everything and I sure hope that they are right. I can't imagine what a world might be like, without my Dad in it, but I know that he would want me to be strong. He would want all of us to continue on, keep are chins up and go and make a difference in the world. Someday we will meet again and on that day, I won't be sad that I'm leaving this world behind. I will be anxiously waiting to see my Dad once again. I love you Dad," she finished.

He sat with his head down looking at his hands folded in his lap. He didn't want anyone to see him, didn't want to talk to anyone. He just wanted to be invisible.

He was amazed at how strong Abigail was at that time. She was definitely, her Father's daughter.

He was shocked by how weak he was and he felt ashamed by it. He thought that if he could see him now, his Dad might be disappointed in him as well. He couldn't bear the thought. He needed to be stronger. He needed to be someone that his Dad could be proud of.

He thought of praying to God to give him strength, but he was furious with Him, and couldn't bring himself to do it. How could he take such a wonderful man such as his Dad? Where was the fairness, the justice in that? He knew his Dad would say things such as; God works in mysterious ways, or that God has a plan for all of us, or that we mustn't question God.

Fuck God. He should have known that the world would be a much better place with his Dad in it. What kind of God lets assholes live and takes good men like his Dad? He broke down and cried again. He felt a twinge of guilt for defying God but he felt that it was deserved all the same.

Abigail fretted over every detail. She was there at every turn, when he needed her she was there. She planned a wonderful wake, full of great food and a live band, but he was in no mood to celebrate his Dad's life. It was custom and he understood that, but It felt like he was celebrating his death and he couldn't bring himself to do it. He felt guilty for that afterwards as well.

"I know, I know, Bill. We all miss him. We never know what the future has in store for us, but he did his very best to prepare us. Now it's our turn, to make our place in the world. Especially you, Bill. You look so much like him and you're a carpenter to boot. You'll be the one to carry our last name forward and I know that you're up to the task," Abigail said.

"I wish that I could be as certain as you. I can't even think right now. I feel like the world that I knew last week, doesn't exist any longer, like I'm empty inside," Bill said.

"Give it some time. You don't have to grow up over night. We're all here for you. Eat something and have a few drinks, it will help."

"Thanks, I'll try."

He forced himself to eat and he did fetch himself a drink as well. That first drink was followed by many others, until for the time being, he had dulled the pain.

He began to withdraw from his sisters. It wasn't a conscious decision. It just happened over the next few months. Abigail tried to visit him as much as possible and his other sisters dropped by, from time to time as well. He was invited to dinners at their houses, frequently at first, but that tapered off after a while. Everyone was busy with their own families and their own grieving. He understood. If truth be told, he just wanted to be left alone most of the time anyway.

He continued going to work every day, but the days dragged by. Without his Dad there to mentor him, to talk to and laugh with, his job felt too much like work. Everything he did and everywhere he went, reminded him of his Dad.

He started going to the pub after work and drinking until he either passed out, or he ran out of money. Occasionally one of his mates would join him but he was mostly alone now.

Six months passed and eventually Abigail had to sell the house and split the money from the estate. She offered him a room at her place and so did Kate, his youngest sister, but he didn't like himself much at the time and he didn't want to burden them with his troubles. He needed to run away, make a fresh start.

He decided to go to America. There he could start over, away from the continual reminder of life before his Dad's death.

CHAPTER THREE

Abigail, Kate, and Margaret met him at the pier, before he boarded the ship to America. Theresa and Nancy couldn't make it but sent small care packages and notes to send him off with. He used his share of his Dad's estate to buy his ticket and there was some left, to help him get a start once he arrived in America. His sisters gave him some other money, that they made him promise to use when he came back to visit them. After he got settled into his new life and could afford to take time away from work, he intended to do just that.

They said their tearful goodbyes and he boarded the ship bound for America. He was excited about his journey and the prospects of a new life, but he was also sad to leave his sisters and his home. For the first time since his Dad's death however, he felt like there was hope of being happy once again.

· · · · ·

He was a very resourceful chap and it didn't take him long to settle in to his new life, make new friends and establish himself. He got a job at the docks unloading ships right away and he rented a room from one of the guys he worked with. He lived there for a couple of months and did small jobs for some of the guys that he worked for. That eventually led to him working for an older gentleman in town making and installing kitchen cabinets and custom carpentry. When the older gentleman retired, he took over the business as a partner and eventually when the old guy died he became the sole proprietor. He named it simply William Johnson's and of course everyone assumed it was named after him, but he knew the truth. He was Bill always was and always would be. He named it after his Dad and he was proud to do so.

He was so busy during this time, that he spent less and less time thinking of his Dad. On rare occasions, he would hear from one of his sisters and that would inevitably get him thinking about him. He found out that, yes it was true that time seemed to heal all wounds and now he could think about his Dad and smile at those memories.

It was also during this time that a friend of his introduced him to a fine young lass named Becky. She was so beautiful, nearly as tall as he was, with the nicest strawberry blonde hair that he had ever seen. He never believed in love at first sight, but that's exactly what it was.

Her family were also Irish immigrants and he was accepted very quickly. After dating for a year and then a short engagement, they were married one cold and blustery, October day. Bill paid for all his sisters to come to the wedding. He used the money that his sisters had given him, plus some of his own that he had been saving. His business was doing well now and he could afford it. He couldn't imagine getting married without all his sisters there, plus, he knew that his Dad would have wanted it that way.

Becky was the absolute love of his life. Her family became his family and her friends became his friends. She was as beautiful inside as she was out. She was as kind a person as you would ever find and smart too. She did have a bit of a temper though and Bill did his best not to provoke her, when she was having one of her days.

She would get mad at him and say things like, "I'd kill ya, if I had the stomach for it!" or "I love ya Bill, but I don't like ya much right now. You best be making yourself scarce, before ya end up buried in the garden. I can't be held accountable, when I'm in a mood."

She would always apologize later. He took no offense to it. He knew she had a temper, that's all.

She was just as quick to compliment him and offer support when he needed it and they could talk about anything, and be themselves. That's what he loved most about her. She was his best friend in the world and he made sure that she knew, and felt it.

"Becky?"

"In here Bill. Just tidying up."

"There you are. I thought I'd finish up early today and take my beautiful wife out for supper."

"You know you don't have to do that, but I love you for it, just the same," she said, showing a devilish little smile.

"Bill, what have you got behind your back? What are you hiding from me?" she asked, laughing, throwing her arms around him and kissing him.

He pulled a bouquet of red, white and yellow roses from behind his back and held them to the side of her face for her to smell.

"They're beautiful."

"Just like you," Bill said.

"You keep saying things like that and you're going to get yourself laid," she said, snatching them from his hand and taking them into the kitchen.

"I love you more today, than the day we were married," she said.

"And I love you. I just wanted to make sure that you knew, that's all. Now, where would you like to go for supper?" Bill asked.

"Not so fast. That can wait," she said, grabbing his hand and leading him into the bedroom.

· · · · ·

He loved her dearly. He wished that his Dad could have met her. He knew that he would have treated her like one of his daughters. That terrible void, when his Dad died, had finally been filled. He had once been his best friend and now Becky assumed that role.

He never knew it was possible, to love someone so completely. He adored her and was a better man, when he was with her.

Becky wanted a large family and they started trying shortly after they were married. Months went by and still they couldn't get pregnant. They went to the doctor and had tests done, but there was nothing that would be preventing them from getting pregnant. They were both fit as fiddles and in the prime of their lives. They continued trying but they focused on themselves and work. They figured if God willed it, then someday they would have many children running around the house.

"We have each other and that's enough for me, Bill, if that's God's will. In the meantime, I don't mind trying," she said, winking at him and running toward the bedroom, removing her blouse as she went.

Bill continued to work hard but he always made time for his new bride.

Shortly after their first anniversary he surprised her with a new house.

"I love our new house and I couldn't be happier," she said, after he took her for a tour.

"I'm glad that you like it."

She spent her time decorating and painting it, just the way they wanted it, until it seemed like home; until it felt just right.

Family and friends were a big part of their life and the extra room that the new house provided was a Godsend.

After his Dad's death, Bill stopped going to church. He was angry with God, for taking him. Becky and her family were Catholics and never missed a Sunday Mass, so Billy joined them. He was a little reluctant at first but he soon forgot about his quarrel with God and started to enjoy going to church again.

Becky and he prayed every night before they went to bed and often they prayed for God to bless them with the pitter patter of little feet, in the halls of their home. One day their prayers were answered.

"I went to my doctor's appointment today. Would you like to know what she said?" she teased.

"Are you serious? You're pregnant?" Bill said, and scooped her into his arms. He cried as he held her tightly.

"You make me so happy. You are going to make the best Mommy in the world."

"And you, are going to make the best Daddy in the world," she said.

"I hope that I can be as good a Father as my Dad was," Bill said, still crying.

"I never met him, but I know that he was a great Father to you and that you will be a great Father to our children. He certainly taught you how to be a good man. I can't wait! I have been praying for this day for so long and I know that you have been too."

"I have, and I can't wait either!" Bill said.

He wished that his Dad was here to share in this wondrous occasion. He called his sisters to tell them the happy news and each of them were so happy, that they cried as well.

Becky had an uneventful pregnancy. She was young, healthy, strong, she ate right and exercised regularly throughout, so they didn't expect any problems when she went into labour.

It was the middle of the night, of course. Becky was prepared however.

"Okay, all my bags for me and the baby are by the front door. There should be two bags. Take them out to the car and then come back to get me. Bill? Did you hear me? Oh, for God's sake Bill. I'm in no shape to be carrying you to the car. Calm down, everything is going to be fine."

"What? No… I'm fine," he said, took a couple of deep breaths and pretended to be calm, for her sake.

They checked her in and took her to the maternity ward. They spent the next few hours watching as her labour progressed normally. The fetal monitor showed that everything was going perfectly until just before they took her into the delivery room. The baby's heart rate started to rise at an alarming rate followed by a sudden crash. The doctor explained that he would have to use forceps to assist and if it was taking too long, then he would have to do an emergency C-section. He helped Becky enough, that the baby was brought into the world at 6:01 A.M. on April 2nd, 1983. He was blue from the umbilical cord being wrapped around his neck. The doctor acted quickly, cutting the cord and freeing him from his entanglement. Immediately he started to turn pink and Becky and Bill cried with relief, but it would be short-lived. The doctor checked his vital signs and said that his pulse was weak. They took him and put him in an incubator and monitored him closely.

"How's our son? Could you go check on him again? I'm so worried. I just want to hold him."

It was hard for Bill to see his tiny son with all the monitors and tubes sticking out of him. He gathered himself before going back to see Becky.

"How is he?" she asked, when he returned.

"He's fine. He's the most beautiful baby that I've ever seen," he said, trying to sound calm.

He prayed to God to let his tiny son live. The doctor told him, that if he made it through the next twenty-four hours, that there was a good chance that he would be just fine. They would continue to monitor him as he got older to make sure that there wasn't permanent damage, caused by the oxygen being cut off to his brain.

Twenty-four excruciating hours passed. Becky and Bill prayed together for their son. Becky slept occasionally but Bill didn't sleep a wink.

Bill prayed sometimes and cursed God at others and then quickly apologized and tried to make amends with Him. He thought that God would probably understand under the circumstances, but he wasn't willing to take any chances.

The next day the doctor brought their baby boy into the room and laid him on Becky's chest. He happily reported that he was doing much better and that his vital signs were right where they should be.

"You have a real fighter on your hands there. Have you given him a name yet?" the doctor asked.

"We didn't name him yet. We wanted to wait, to make sure that he was going to be alright. We are going to name him Billy Pope Johnson after his Grandfather," Becky said.

"That's a good solid name," the doctor replied.

Bill thought of his Dad and how proud he would be to have a grandson named after him. He wished that he was here to share in this happy occasion.

"He's perfect, Bill. Look at his little hands, they're so tiny," she said, caressing him.

Bill fell asleep with a smile on his face, watching Becky bond with their baby boy. He napped only briefly, while they waited for Becky and Billy to be released by the doctor. He was on top of the world. He should have been unbelievably tired but his excitement kept him going. He took Becky and his new son home and they settled into their new life.

A year later they were back at the same hospital welcoming their second son into the world. They named him Henry David Johnson after Becky's Dad.

Life was incredible and he couldn't have planned a better life for himself. He had a beautiful loving wife and two healthy, happy kids. Billy didn't show any ill-effects from the trouble he had encountered during his birth. Bill himself, tried to be a good Father and husband, and for the most part he succeeded.

This is where the happy story of Bill and his young family started to unravel.

Becky started feeling tired all the time. She went to the doctor and had tests done but she couldn't find anything wrong with her. Bill didn't need a doctor to tell him that his beautiful wife was ill. She was usually so full of energy, and now she just didn't seem herself. She developed dark circles under her eyes and her appetite wasn't what it used to be. At first they hoped that she was just run down from chasing two toddlers all the time, but as time went on, they knew that it was something more.

Three months went by, Becky saw the doctor several times and each time she couldn't find anything wrong with her. Finally, they decided to get a second opinion and that's when they found she had cancer.

Bill tried to remain positive, but he was worried that he might lose the love of his life. He put on a brave face for Becky and he said all the right things, but the truth of it was, that he was scared to death of what lie ahead.

The doctor explained the treatment regimen that she would follow, which included chemotherapy and surgery to remove a tumour on her lung. As Becky got sicker, Bill fell deeper and deeper into despair. He tried to stay strong for Becky and the children, but it became increasingly more difficult with time.

Becky did rebound a couple of times and they thought that she might be okay, but she soon became sick again. Bill spent as much time with his ailing wife as he could and his carpentry business started to falter, as a result. They had to re-mortgage their home to pay for the mounting medical bills but it still wasn't enough. Bill kept it all from Becky, because he didn't want to worry her.

"Bill, I know you're a good Father. I know that you'll take care of our boys when I'm gone. Tell them that I love them and that I'm sorry for leaving them," Becky said.

"You can tell them yourself. You can beat this."

"We both know, that's not true, but I love you for trying," she said, squeezing his hand and smiling.

She died quietly in Bill's arms and he held her tightly and cried until there were no tears left. He felt as though his heart had been ripped from his chest. Even the passing of his Dad, paled in comparison to the despair that he now felt. He had many months to get ready, and he knew this day would come, that it was inevitable, but nothing could have prepared him for this moment. He was drained, exhausted, but most of all, it felt as though he would die from a broken heart.

He sleepwalked through the next few months. He buried the love of his life and he lost his beautiful home. He lost his will to live. He tried to be strong for his young children, but he felt lost. He felt like a failure and he didn't know where to go, or what to do.

He didn't have enough money to buy a house in the city, so he packed up their belongings and moved with the kids to a small town a few miles away. He put a meager deposit down, on a tiny house, which was more of a shack, really.

He hadn't talked to his sisters in months. He couldn't face them. He knew that he had to provide for his two boys but he hurt so badly; he didn't think he could continue. Old habits surfaced and he began to spend more time at the local bar. The only time that he didn't hurt was when he was drunk. He drank when the kids were at day-care and he drank afterwards when the children were home with him.

He felt disgusted with himself and he knew that his Dad would be ashamed with the man that he had become. He couldn't stop the hurting and he was on a downward spiral, that he just couldn't stop.

All his hopes of being a wonderful father like his Dad, were lost and eventually he was completely lost himself.

CHAPTER FOUR

Billy and Henry grew up completely different than their Dad. Their Dad had a wonderful upbringing surrounded by close family. He had a Father that he could be proud of, and look up to. Billy and Henry's Dad was a drunk and a terrible father. He was lost and hurting and he couldn't find the strength to change his position in life. Billy and Henry didn't know any of that. All they knew was what they saw for most of their young lives. They saw a broken man, that left Billy to watch out and care for his younger brother.

Billy was nine years old, far too young to be looking after his brother and certainly too young to be looking after his Dad as well. But, that's exactly the position that he found himself in. He never knew his Mom, she died when he was still too young. He did know that his Dad was no good and he wasn't someone to be proud of. He knew that he and Henry, had to stick together.

He tried to be good so that his Dad wouldn't be mad at him, but it never seemed to be enough. No matter how hard he tried, his Dad seemed to always be angry. He was mad at the world and at God.

Billy sometimes wished that his Dad would die. He thought that he and Henry would be better off without him. They looked after themselves most of the time anyway. They didn't need him.

Child protective services came to the house several times. The lady that came to visit them seemed nice and she smelled really good too. She had a lot of questions to ask him and Henry, and they did their best to answer them all.

"How are you boys doing? Is everything okay with your Father? I mean, has he stopped his drinking?" she asked.

"He doesn't drink in front of us any more. He goes to the bar and drinks by himself, mostly," Henry answered.

"What he meant to say, is that he has a couple of drinks with his friends, once in a while," Billy said.

"He leaves you boys here, all alone?"

"Yeah, but we know better than to get into trouble. We ain't toddlers," Billy said.

"Oh, my God! And does he make you supper every night?"

"Sometimes, but we like making our own supper, anyway. That way we can have what we want, and we don't have to eat any vegetables," Henry said.

"Thanks boys. I think that I've heard enough. I have to talk to your Father now."

"Did we do something wrong? Are you mad at us?" Henry asked.

"Oh, no dear. You haven't done anything wrong and I could never be mad at you two, sweetheart," she said.

She gave them each a hug and then went to talk to their Dad. Billy and Henry couldn't hear what she was saying to him, but they could sure hear his response.

"You have no right to tell me how to raise my children! We're doing just fine! Aren't we boys?" he said looking in their direction.

Henry and Billy nodded in agreement.

"Now, get out of here and don't come back," he yelled, and then turned and stumbled toward the front door.

Billy felt really bad. He didn't understand how his Dad could be so mean to her. She was always so nice, when she came to visit.

Shortly after that, the nice lady came back, only this time she brought two policemen with her. She explained to him and Henry that they were going to live with a real nice family, that was going to look after them while their Dad got some help.

The man and woman that took Billy and Henry in, were very nice, like the Lady said that they would be. They took Henry and Billy to the park, rode bikes with them, took them fishing, all kinds of fun stuff. Billy and Henry liked them very much but they still felt a connection to their Dad for some reason.

Their Dad would meet them at the nice lady's office once a week. They would visit for a while and then she would take them back to where they had been living. This continued for six months or so, until the nice lady said that they were going back to live with their Dad again.

Billy felt torn between his Dad and the nice couple that had been looking after him and his kid brother. There was no question who treated them better, but he still felt loyalty toward his Dad.

Their Dad stopped drinking and he spent more time with Billy and Henry. He did things with them and he looked after them better, but Billy could tell that his Dad was very unhappy. He seldom smiled and he looked tired all the time. Billy wondered what made his Dad so sad most of the time and he wondered if it had to do with his Mom.

"Hey Dad, can you tell Henry and me about our Mom? What was she like?" Billy asked one night as they were eating their supper.

His Dad's eyes lit up for the briefest of moments before becoming dark once again. A fleeting smile crossed his lips and then it was gone. He began to speak slowly but the more he spoke the faster he got.

"Oh… my Becky. She was smart, funny and beautiful. She challenged me like no one else ever had. She had a strong will, but even that couldn't beat the cancer. I was so happy to call her my wife and the Mother of my children. She had a fiery temper but she was quick to apologize and she never held a grudge. She loved you boys so much and she told me to look after you and tell you just how much she loved you."

Billy couldn't ever remember his Dad speaking her name before. It was like a flood gate had been opened. He'd never heard him speak so much, and for so long as he did then. He talked at great length about his Mom, and then he continued to tell him and Henry about how great a man that their Grandfather was as well. This was as close to happy as Billy had ever seen him, but when he finished telling his story, his eyes went dark again and the smile faded from his lips.

"I'm so sorry boys. I wanted to be a good father like my Dad was to me. He and your Mom would be so ashamed of who I have become. I'm going to try to be a better father, I promise," he said.

He tried. Billy and Henry could see the difference, but they could still see the sadness in their Father and it made Billy feel a little sad as well. He wished that he could have known his Mom, she sounded like a wonderful person. Billy had a picture of her in his room and he often picked it up off his night stand and looked at it when he had trouble sleeping. She looked so beautiful and kind and she always helped him to get back to sleep.

Billy always felt like there was something missing and after he heard the stories about his Mom and Grandfather, that feeling grew. Billy still spent almost every moment of his free time with his kid brother Henry. Their Dad was making a real effort to be a better father, but years of Billy and Henry having to fend for themselves, had left its mark.

Billy didn't have much figured out and he only knew how to survive in his small little world. He did know a couple of things though. He felt better when he was in control of a situation, instead of being at the mercy of circumstance. He also knew, that there seemed to be something missing inside of him. He didn't know exactly what it was, but he discovered that he could fill that void and he knew that it made him feel better; a whole lot better.

One day he was at the play park with Henry, which wasn't unusual, because he and Henry went there all the time. This particular time was different, however. There was another little boy there and he was playing with a magnifying glass, focusing the sun's rays and burning leaves.

"Can I try it?" Billy asked.

"I just got it for my birthday, from my parents. I'd rather not," he said, pulling it back and holding it tightly to his chest.

Billy didn't think that there was a story behind why the boy wouldn't share. All he knew, was that he was being quite rude. He had asked him nicely enough. Billy was pretty sure, that he would have let the little boy borrow his, if he had one of his own. He thought that perhaps a rude little boy such as this, didn't deserve such a cool toy.

"I just want to try. I'll give it right back, I promise," Billy pleaded.

"I don't think so. I don't think it would be a good idea to lend it to a stranger," the little boy said.

"My name's Billy, and this here is my kid brother Henry. What's your name?" he asked, motioning with his thumb to Henry standing beside him, as he spoke.

"My name is Oliver," he said.

"Well, hello Oliver. It's nice to meet you," Billy said.

"Yeah, nice to meet you Oliver," Henry said.

"See we ain't strangers anymore," Billy said.

"I'm sorry, but I don't think I should. My Dad would be mad at me if he found out," Oliver said, meekly.

"No one is going to find out. How would he know?" Billy asked.

"My sister is just over there. She would tattle for sure. She likes getting me in trouble," Oliver said.

Billy had enough of trying to persuade Oliver to let him take a turn. He felt a red, fiery anger, flash within him. He grabbed the magnifying glass from him and pushed him to the ground.

"Now see what you made me do. I just wanted to take a turn, but no, that wasn't good enough. Now I have to take it for myself."

"Come on Henry, let's get out of here," Billy said.

"But Billy, I don't think that you ought to be doin' that. You might get us in trouble. Besides, it's not very nice," Henry said.

That anger rose in him again, and he spun to face Henry. Henry took a step backward. He had never seen that look in his brother's eyes before.

"Listen! I'm older than you. I've looked after you this far, haven't I? Now, stop your belly-aching and let's get outta here," Billy said.

Billy knew what Henry was thinking. It was wrong, and that he didn't like it. Billy was sure that Henry could see the look in his eyes and he guessed that he didn't like it all that much either. Billy could get bossy from time to time, but this was something different. Henry started to say something, thought better of it, and just followed him from the park and down the little trail and into the woods.

Henry looked back to where Oliver was lying in the dirt crying. Billy could see the pained look on his face, when he turned back around.

"Are you goin' to keep up? We gotta get outta here before he tattles on us," Billy said.

Billy stopped several hundred yards into the woods, in a bit of a clearing. He wanted to try out his new toy. He knelt on the edge of the path and focused the beam of light on a leaf like he had seen Oliver do. Henry knelt beside him. Billy was smiling from ear to ear, but Henry was still pouting.

"That wasn't very nice; what you did to Oliver," Henry said, but Billy just ignored him.

The leaf smoked for quite a while, until a small breeze blew cross- ways and ignited it. Billy laughed with delight and even Henry had to smile a little. They watched the leaf burn itself out and then a line of ants caught Billy's attention. He focused the beam on one of the ants and immediately it began to curl up. Its legs burned off its small body, it began to shrivel and then crackle.

Billy was delighted. He was very satisfied with himself. He felt something inside that he had never felt before. He didn't know exactly what to make of it, or how to describe it. He focused the beam of the magnifying glass on another ant and then another and another. Each time he felt a small, almost imperceptible feeling. He knew it was crazy, but it was almost as though he could feel the ants' pain, feel their terror, and he liked it. He liked it a lot as a matter of fact. It felt as though the empty void that was inside of him was starting to fill and he was somehow more whole than he had ever been. He wanted to try something bigger, just to make sure he wasn't imagining things. He felt a little conflicted at the same time. He knew what he had done with Oliver was wrong and he knew what he was doing now was wrong, but it felt too good. Just a little more and then he would stop.

He found his next target only a few feet away. A fuzzy black and orange caterpillar crept along the side of the path. Billy knelt in front of it and focused a beam of light at a spot in the sand, in front of the caterpillar's intended path.

"Don't Billy! It's so pretty. You shouldn't do that, it's not nice," Henry said.

"Shut up Henry! It's not hurting anything!"

"It'll hurt the caterpillar," Henry said.

"Yeah but they don't feel pain the same way that we do," Billy explained.

"I don't know a lot about caterpillars, but I think all of God's creatures feel pain," he said, and then added. "Besides, it just isn't right."

"I know the difference between right and wrong and I'm tellin' you, they don't feel pain, so drop it!"

Billy kept the light focused on the sand directly in front of the caterpillar and it slowly moved right towards it. It hesitated for a moment and Henry hoped that it would change course and be saved, but then it continued, into the beam of light. It moved under the focused rays, slowed and then stopped. The furry part of it began to burn and melt. A small wisp of smoke rose from it. It began to writhe and squirm and Billy held the beam steady on the side of it, until it stopped moving and seemed to shrivel in on its self and then turn to charred dust. Billy set the magnifying glass aside and inhaled deeply and rose his arms to the sky, as if he was praising God for this moment.

"Ahh, that's the stuff," he said, with a pleased look on his face.

He laughed, picked up the magnifying glass and jumped to his feet.

"God's going to be mad at you for killing one of his beautiful creatures," Henry said defiantly. "I'm going to pray for you tonight, before bed."

"Suit yourself," Billy said, smugly.

Billy was on top of the world. He had an extra spring in his step the rest of the day. He was in as good a mood as he could ever remember. Billy even took Henry to the Tasty Treat and bought him an ice cream. Henry loved ice cream, but he very seldom ever got it. He loved his brother for buying him that wonderful, tasty ice cream. Maybe, Billy wasn't so bad after all.

Billy couldn't believe the feeling that he got when he burned the caterpillar. He tried to hide his feelings the best he could from his kid brother, but he found it hard to do. He felt a little guilty at first but the feeling that he got, far out-weighed the guilt. He could feel the pain that the caterpillar felt. He wasn't sure with the ants because they were so small, but now he was positive, that he wasn't just imagining it. The feeling was there, as plain as day. He knew that it was scared as well, and he could feel the moment that it died. He felt, like the life that faded from the caterpillar was transferred to him somehow.

He thought back to taking the magnifying glass from Oliver. That was the start of it. He dismissed it at the time, but he could feel what Oliver was feeling. He could feel his misery, his despair, his hopelessness and anger. It buoyed his spirits and made him feel better, less empty. It filled him up. That was it! It filled him up! The emotion and life that he took from others, filled him up! He didn't know how it worked or why, but he liked the feeling, he liked it a lot. He would have to conduct some more experiments of course, but that was something, that he was looking forward to doing.

CHAPTER FIVE

Billy cried for several minutes and his sense of despair slowly faded away. He gathered himself, and even though there was no one on the mountain to see his most recent melt down, he was embarrassed all the same. He tried to adjust his position and found that he was still unable to move. The parts that were hurt, screamed with pain and the parts that weren't, were numb from lying in the same position, for far too long. The only saving grace was that it meant that he was still alive. He was certainly happy about that and hoped it would remain that way. He wondered at what point a person would be happy to die. He guessed that it was different for everyone but he knew that for him, that point was still a long way off.

For now, he was content to watch the sun climb in the sky. He was thankful for small things at this point, it was all that he had. He was thankful that the long, dark night was behind him and the new one was still hours away. Every minute brought with it the chance, that someone would cross the mountain and rescue him from his misery.

All he had, was time to think, to remember and regret. The top of his list was his brother Henry. He loved Henry, but he didn't know how much until after he was gone. He protected Henry from many things and many people, but the one person he couldn't protect him from, was himself.

"I'm sorry Henry. I'm so sorry. If I could trade places with you I would, I swear I would," he said to the mountain.

The leaves in the trees rustled and whispered back their disapproval.

"Liar, liar, liar," they repeated, in their hushed voices, until he thought that he would go mad.

"Shut up! Shut up!" he screamed at them, but they continued to whisper.

Henry didn't deserve what had happened to him. Billy deserved to die, not Henry, he knew that, but that didn't diminish his will to live. He wanted to live as much as anyone, only, they had everything to live for. They had loved ones waiting for them to come home to, that would miss them and would grieve for them, when they didn't. He had no such person waiting for him at home. No one that would care that he hadn't returned. That wasn't true and he knew it. He just didn't think that he deserved it.

If only he could have controlled his new-found thirst, his addiction. He couldn't believe the monster that he had become, that he could do the things he had done, what he had done to Henry. He looked up to him, trusted him, and look how he repaid him.

CHAPTER SIX

Billy had just discovered that he could feel others' pain and that it filled him up like nothing else could. It was like a drug that he just couldn't get enough of. It was destructive and he knew that now, but at the time it consumed him and he wasn't thinking clearly.

Billy and Henry were waiting on the bridge in the woods one day.

"I don't want to do this. Let's do something else," Henry whined.

"We're just going to have a little harmless fun. No one's going to get hurt, just scared a little," Billy said, smiling

"I don't think it's fun," Henry said, and shoved his hands in his pockets.

Billy wasn't in the mood to listen to Henry try to ruin his fun, so he just tuned him out. Terrorizing kids filled him up almost as much as hurting them, but It became harder and harder for him to get the same satisfaction. Henry became increasingly critical of Billy's actions and he became more vocal about it as time passed. Billy became weary of Henry's protestations and he had nearly enough of it.

"Here comes that fat kid, Jack, I think his name is. He should be a good one. He's always fun to pick on; he gets all blubbery and scared. Just follow my lead Henry," Billy said.

"Okay," Henry said, staring at the ground.

"Oh look! He has a nice, shiny, Scooby-doo lunch box and a new hat by the looks of it. Should be easy to get him going," Billy said, completely ignoring the fact that Henry was upset.

"Hey fatty!" Billy called out.

Jack continued to trudge along. Billy wasn't sure if he didn't hear him, or if he was just ignoring him. Billy felt the anger rising in him, something that had been happening more frequently lately. His desire to feel the rush of other people's emotions drove him more than anything at the moment, and anyone that stood in his way, felt his wrath.

"Hey fatty, I'm talking to you," Billy called to him, from his perch atop the railing.

Jack kept trudging toward the bridge.

"Are you hard of hearing or just stupid?" Billy yelled at him.

"I don't want any trouble. I just want to get to school," he said, meekly.

"No problem, but if you want to cross the bridge, you'll have to pay the toll," Billy said.

"I don't have any money," he said, and kept walking.

He was nearly at the bridge now and Billy jumped down from the railing to block his way.

"If you want to pass, you'll have to give Henry there a blowjob," Billy said, motioning toward his brother.

"Leave him alone Billy, he didn't do anything to you," Henry pleaded.

"Shut the fuck up Henry, or when I'm done beatin' the shit out of fatty here, it'll be your turn!" Billy yelled.

His face was red and he spat when he yelled. He pumped the fist of his right hand up and down in a hammering motion.

Henry got down slowly from his perch atop the railing of the bridge. When he reached the ground, he stood with his hands in his pockets, staring downward.

"I think we should just let him be, Billy," Henry said quietly, as he kicked at the stones lining the path, with his sneaker.

Billy took three quick strides across the path and punched Henry in the mouth before he had time to move. Henry went sprawling backwards, landing on his back in the grass, alongside the path. Blood trickled from his right nostril and from the corner of his mouth. Henry reached up to wipe at the blood. Tears began to run down his face and he sniffled from the blood and snot collecting in his nose. He spat a large mixture of blood and saliva onto the path in front of him. He lay there looking up at Billy, a hurt look painted painfully across his face.

"Now look what you made me do. You think I like hitting my younger brother? All you have to do is listen once in a while," Billy said, extending his hand to help Henry to his feet.

Henry slowly reached up and grabbed hold of Billy's hand. His cheek was all red and puffy, but he had stopped crying. He got to his feet and stood looking at the ground again.

Billy felt a twinge of regret for hitting his brother, but he resented Henry for trying to interfere with him feeding his new-found obsession.

While he was thinking, Jack started to walk toward the bridge again. Billy swung in his direction and he stopped in his tracks. He had a scared look on his face that delighted Billy.

"Where you going, you fat fuck?" Billy screamed.

"I have to go to school," he said, still snivelling.

"You're not going anywhere, until you pay the fuckin' toll."

"I'm not giving Henry a blowjob," he said, crying now.

Billy didn't really expect him to and he wouldn't have made Henry go through with it anyway, but he wanted Jack to think that he would.

"Well then, you're going to have to give us something," Billy said, plucking the hat from his head, faster than a cat catching a mouse.

"Hey, give me that back," he protested.

"This is one smart hat, isn't it Henry?" Billy said, while loosening the strap on the back.

"Sure is Billy," Henry said, eyes still a little downcast.

"This fucking thing is too small. Here you try it," he said, as he threw it to Henry.

Henry tried it on half-heartedly and then held it out to Jack. He went to grab for it but Billy hit his arm down, out of the way.

"It's of no use to us. Go ahead and piss in it Henry."

Henry started to grumble, but thought better of it. Henry threw the hat on the ground and pissed in it. There was a large puddle of urine pooled in the upside-down hat.

"Now put your hat back on, you fat fuck!" Billy roared.

Jack started to cry again, to the delight of Billy. He could feel the sadness and despair that Jack was experiencing, and he loved it.

"Put it on!" Billy yelled.

He slowly lifted the hat. Urine ran down his hand and wrist as he slowly lowered it unto his head. Billy laughed gleefully, clapping his hands together and shot a quick glance in Henry's direction. Henry was still standing with his head down and his shoulders hunched, looking fixedly at the ground.

"Now give me your lunch box. It doesn't look like you need to eat, anyway," Billy snarled.

Jack slowly handed him his lunch box and stood there looking down at the ground, in much the same manner as Henry.

Billy opened the lunch box to examine its contents. There was a peanut butter and jelly sandwich, an apple, a granola bar and a juice box inside. Billy took a bite of the apple and threw it into the river. He put the rest of the stuff in his pockets. He threw the lunch box to the ground and stomped on it with both feet. He jumped on it several times until it was smashed into a hundred pieces. He looked up at Jack and smiled crazily. He was very pleased with himself.

"I don't want no stupid Scooby-Doo lunch box. That's for dumb kids like you. Now get the fuck out of here, before I beat you within an inch of your life. And don't be tattlin' on us, or you'll get it worse next time," Billy said.

Billy started laughing hysterically. He could feel himself filling up. That was just what the doctor ordered. He felt on top of the world.

"I thought you were going to school?" Billy called after him, laughing all the while.

Billy watched as Jack ran down the path and out of sight, enjoying the moment. He took a deep breath and savoured the last few seconds of feelings rushing in, and then turned toward Henry.

"Why couldn't you just go along with it as I asked? That fuckin' space cadet got what was coming to him. You're too soft Henry. You need to toughen up if you're going to make it in this world," Billy said.

Henry didn't say anything.

"I'm sorry for hitting you Henry."

"It's okay," Henry said.

·   ·   ·   ·   ·

It was one year later when Billy and Jack crossed paths once again. Billy had tormented him since then but it usually didn't amount to much, until this day.

Billy stood in front of Jack and blocked his way as he tried to walk past. He yelled at him but Jack ignored him and kept silent.

"Can you hear me, space cadet?" Billy yelled, while drops of spit sprayed across Jack's face.

Jack wiped it from his lips.

"Are you fuckin' deaf or just stupid, or maybe both?" Billy asked.

Jack continued to look down at his feet and a small smirk escaped the corners of his mouth. Billy flew into a rage at the sight of him smiling.

"I'm talking to you space cadet, and you'd better fuckin' answer me, or I swear I'm going to fuck you up real bad!" he yelled.

Billy had worked himself into a bit of a frenzy by this point and it didn't matter what Jack did or didn't do. Billy was beyond the point of reason. He took one quick step forward and punched Jack hard in the mouth with his right fist. He went reeling backwards and would have surely smashed his head on the curb behind him if, it weren't for Henry catching him. Blood spilled from both nostrils and a large split opened in his upper lip. He spat a large mass of blood and saliva onto the sidewalk beside him and then looked back, through tear blurred eyes, toward where Billy had been standing. Billy was no longer standing there. He had moved to beside him and Henry. Henry let him fall to the ground as gently as he could and then turned to face his older brother. Billy's face was twisted with rage. His face was blood red and he was panting wildly. He charged forward, like a bull charging a matador. He meant to tackle Henry to the ground and lay a beating on him, but he never got the chance. Billy was still charging forward with his arms outstretched in front of him, reaching for Henry's waist. Henry pistoned his left leg up hard and caught Billy flush in the face. It wasn't clear if it was just a reaction or if Henry had finally had enough of Billy's bullying over the years, but the result, was the same. Billy's broken nose sprayed blood down his face and all over Henry's jeans, and a few droplets found their way to the left shoulder of Jack's t-shirt. Billy collapsed in a heap, unconscious. Henry and Jack looked at each other with shocked looks on their faces. Henry turned back toward his brother and knelt beside him. He put his ear beside his face and listened for the sound of him breathing.

"He's okay, just unconscious. Boy, is he gonna be pissed when he comes to. You had better not be here when he does. I'll stay to make sure he's okay, but you'd better bugger off," Henry said.

"I think you're right. Thanks, Henry."

"Don't mention it. He had it coming to him," he said, and then turned to Billy again.

"You going to be alright?"

"I'll be fine. I don't think he'll be up for another round, when he wakes up."

"I'm just thinking about later, once he recovers."

"Just go, I'll be okay," Henry said shrugging his shoulders, and Jack turned and walked away.

Billy stirred from beside him and Henry looked down to see his eyes fluttering. Billy moaned and reached up to examine his broken nose with his fingertips. After he had assessed the damage, he opened his eyes and looked at Henry.

"Don't just sit there, help me up!" he ordered.

Henry did as he was asked. If the truth be told, he felt a little guilty for having knocked Billy out. It was never his intention to hurt his big brother, he didn't like hurting anyone or anything. It was just a reaction, pure and simple.

"I guess little brother is all grown up. You caught me off guard, but it won't happen again, so you had better watch yourself in the future," Billy said.

Billy talked a big game but their relationship would be forever changed, from that incident on. Billy's voice didn't have the same conviction that it did before. The words sounded like something that Billy would say, but they were hollow and without substance.

The next few weeks were a strange time, Billy wasn't himself. He acted sullen and distant, even his new addiction was put on the back burner for now. Henry didn't like who his brother had become, but the way he was acting now scared him even more. Billy rarely smiled, hardly even talked for that matter. He kept to himself, went off on his own more often, and didn't invite Henry along.

Billy was in a bit of a funk, there was no denying it. It started when Henry stood up to him and knocked his ass out, but that wasn't it. He couldn't put his finger on it and he spent a good deal of his time thinking about it, but just couldn't explain his mood as of late.

The high that he had felt when he tormented Jack and others was missing. It didn't fill him up any more, and he felt empty.

That was it! His ah ha moment. His moment of recognition. Finally, he had identified the cause of the funk he was in. He needed to get out there and fill himself up, only from now on, he was going to leave Henry out of it. There was no room for him in his new plans. Henry would only bring him down.

CHAPTER SEVEN

Billy was used to having Henry around all the time and he leaned on him more than he cared to admit, but this was something that he needed to do on his own. His new addiction however, clouded his judgement and made him do things that he would never have dreamt of doing before. None of this happened over night. It took some time for him to work his way up to that point.

Billy realized that killing insects and terrorizing kids on the playground weren't doing it for him any longer. It didn't fill him up like it once did. The empty, hollow feeling had returned and he needed to fill it.

He needed to find larger prey, something with more capacity to fill the void. He walked aimlessly through the streets and through wooded areas on the edge of town, but nothing presented itself as a suitable candidate, for his next experiment.

He trudged lethargically back home, went to his room and closed his door on the world. His spirits were at an all-time low. He turned the T.V. on, trying to distract his thoughts, but it was of no use. He curled up in his bed and stared at the wall. There were no thoughts, no plans, just a grey, dull absence that over took him. He was lonely and depressed and he saw no way to move forward.

Eventually the boredom overtook him and merciful sleep, took him away from his troubled life.

He dreamt of his Grandfather and of his Mom, who he never knew. In his dream, he was happy for a fleeting moment and then he became sullen, and dark circles appeared under his eyes, that were no longer blue. Wrinkles appeared at the corners, he was bent over at the waist and held a cane in his right hand. His hair had whitened and thinned and he wore glasses on his face. Dark age spots blotched his previously smooth, white skin. He grimaced at the sight of it and was taken aback by the yellow teeth protruding from beneath his cracked lips. They were filed to points, and red, puffy gums swelled from between them. A constant high-pitched hum, filled his ears and there was an ever-present rattle in his chest.

A large snapping sound chased away the droning hum from his ears. The blotches on his skin quickly faded away and his teeth and gums returned to their previous condition. His hair filled in and was replaced by long flowing locks of thick brown hair. He threw the cane to the corner of the room along with the glasses from his face and stood upright. A wonderful, warm, comforting feeling washed over him, filling him up. The sense of despair and hollowness was replaced with a happy, almost giddy feeling of joy and fullness.

He awoke from his dream to the sound of squealing coming from the corner of his room. He leapt from his bed and hit the light switch on the wall. He hurried in the direction of the sound and found a rat caught in a trap, that had been strategically placed by his father. The bar of the trap had caught the rat by the front leg and it struggled to escape, squealing all the while.

Billy knelt on the floor by its side.

"I can feel your pain little guy. I know that you are hurting and I know that you are scared, but I'm sorry to say, that I'm not going to be able to put you out of your misery. Not just yet anyway. I still have some filling up to do," Billy said.

Billy inhaled deeply and let the wonderful feeling wash over him. He felt so alive, so fulfilled, so free and strong. The hollow feeling that had plagued him over the last month was gone and he felt complete once again.

When the feeling felt as though it started to level off, he brought his foot down hard atop the rat in the trap. He liked the feeling he got from the struggling rat, but he also knew right from wrong and it would be wrong to let the rat suffer needlessly.

The moment he brought his foot down on top of the rat and extinguished his life, an explosion filled his mind. The struggling rat had filled his body, filled his soul, but this was different. It was as though an electric current had passed through his brain and he felt more alive than he had ever felt before. He laughed out loud, with sheer delight. A smile spread across his face, so wide that it hurt. He felt like he would explode from the happiness that he felt inside. He spun around in circles with his arms flung out to his sides. He had to move, he couldn't stay still. It felt as though there was more energy in him than he could withstand.

He ran from his bedroom, out the front door, down the street and into the woods. He spun and laughed and ran and jumped, until finally the feeling subsided and he slowed to a brisk walk. The large grin still went from ear to ear. The feeling lessened a little, but it was still lurking beneath the surface. He felt better than ever before, on top of the world, and nothing or no one could take this feeling from him.

He made his way back to the house and slipped quietly into his room. He lay on his bed, but it was impossible to sleep and he had no desire to do so. It was as if an electric current still pulsed through his body. All his senses seemed to be heightened or enhanced. He couldn't wipe the stupid grin from his face. He lay there looking at the ceiling, the thoughts of misery and despair, long forgotten.

He never slept a wink the rest of the night, and in the morning, he emerged from his room, not tired but on top of the world, with an extra spring in his step.

"What's up with you?" Henry asked, while they ate their cereal.

"Nothing. Why, what do you mean?"

"You've been miserable for weeks, today you wake up and you're smiling and whistling like an idiot. Something must have changed."

"Had a good night. Just sorted through some stuff that's all," Billy said.

"Whatever. Don't tell me then, I don't care, as long as you aren't moping around here anymore," Henry said.

"No, no more moping for this cat!" Billy said, and smiled even wider.

"Okay, if you say so, but it's kinda creepy if you ask me."

Henry took one final look over his shoulder at his brother as he put his bowl in the sink and then went to get dressed for school.

When he finished, he came out into the hallway and Billy was waiting for him. He reminded Henry of his old dog Scout, who used to bounce beside him waiting to be played with. Billy had that same energy about him today.

"What do you say we skip school today? There's no way I can sit in class all day, I have to keep moving. Let's go do something, we haven't hung out in a long time. Just you and me, the two of us against the world, like old times. What do you say? I know I've been a bit of a shmuck lately, but I feel much better now," Billy asked eagerly.

"Sure Billy, what do you have in mind?" Henry asked, hesitantly.

"Nothing really, I just know I can't be in school right now. Hey, what do you say we go fishing?"

"Sure that's fine by me."

Their Dad had already left for work, so they were free to get their fishing rods and tackle from the shed. They still snuck down to the river, for fear of someone seeing them and telling their Dad. Once they were in the clear, Billy's bubbly mood returned once again. Apparently, his mood had started to wear off on Henry, because he was now smiling and whistling as well.

"Hey, Billy what's changed?" he asked quietly.

"Huh? What was that? I was lost in thought."

"Nothing. It doesn't matter," Henry said, putting his arm around Billy.

Billy put his arm over Henry's shoulders, and they walked like that, the rest of the way to the stream.

They spent the day fishing, goofing off and enjoying each other's company. They caught a couple of beautiful rainbow trout, that they released to catch another day.

The day wasn't about the fishing though. It was more about two brothers hanging out and having a good time. Billy's mood continued to border on giddy all day and they had one of the best times that they could ever remember.

Billy's mood held for the better part of two weeks. He was still in good spirits for another week and then an okay mood for awhile before the darkness began to creep in again. His mood changed slowly, imperceptibly, but after another week it was unmistakable. It wasn't only his mood that changed. He had a different look about him as well. He looked older, more tired. Dark circles began to appear beneath his eyes again and the smile that was ever-present, was absent once again.

Billy began keeping to himself and had no desire to hang out with Henry any longer. Any time that Henry tried to talk to him, Billy became upset, almost violent at times.

"What's gotten into you? You were fun again for a while and now you're acting strangely again. You look different too. Are you alright? Are you sick or something?" Henry asked.

"I'm fine. I just don't want to be bothered by a stupid little kid all the time.

Don't you have any friends your own age?" Billy snarled.

"You don't seem fine. You're acting like a real jerk," Henry said, and went into his room and closed the door.

The weather turned from hot, to hotter than Hell during this time and the only reprieve was the local quarry where they could go for a swim to cool off. It was Saturday and their Dad was finishing up a couple of small jobs in town. Billy wanted to go swimming to cool off and he wanted to go by himself.

"That's fine, but you have to take Henry with you."

"Come on! I never get to go anywhere without him hanging on me."

"That's the deal. Take it or leave it."

"I'll take it, I guess," he grumbled.

The hollowness had returned and it was getting worse by the day. He had hoped that it would pass, but he now realized that there was only one way to get rid of it. He needed to fill up again and he didn't want Henry interfering with his plans. He just wanted to be left alone all the time now. The first time he felt like this it was bad, but this time, it felt as though it was getting worse. The hollow feeling, the anxiousness and despair seemed to be growing by the day; hell, by the minute. He felt like he was about to lose his mind, like he was about to crack. He didn't want Henry to see him like this, but more importantly he didn't want Henry to try and stop him, from what he needed to do. Henry was too soft, too caring. Billy wasn't a monster, but he knew what needed to be done. He didn't have a choice in the matter and he intended to do, whatever it took.

Billy and Henry walked in relative silence, the two miles to the quarry on the edge of town. Billy didn't feel like talking and Henry looked as though he was afraid to. By the time they got there they were both drenched in sweat and they needed to cool off badly. The cool water lay some sixty feet below the edge of the steep cliffs of the quarry. Its shimmering, blue water looked cool and inviting, and Henry couldn't wait to get there. Billy however was distracted by something he saw at the top of the cliff.

"Hey wait Henry! There's something there in the grass," Billy said, pointing in front of him.

Billy walked over and bent down in the tall grass. Henry went to see what he was looking at, and discovered that there was a baby bunny nestled there.

"Aww, look how cute he is," Henry said.

Billy didn't notice. All he could think about was, how hurting this bunny would fill him up. He reached out slowly and the bunny hunkered down in the tall grass, trying to hide. Billy grabbed him by the neck, pulled him free from the grass and held him out in front of him.

"Let him go! You're going to hurt him," Henry cried.

Billy ignored him and tightened his grip around the defenseless bunny's neck.

"Let him go!" Henry yelled this time, but Billy continued to ignore him.

Henry reached for the bunny to try and pry him from Billy's hands, but he held him just out of reach. Henry became desperate.

"You're going to kill him! You're choking him! Let him go!"

He hit Billy's arms, but still he continued to strangle the bunny. An eerie smile began to creep across his face. The dark circles were beginning to fade from beneath his eyes.

Henry kicked Billy as hard as he could in the ribs and he immediately dropped the bunny, and grabbed at them. The bunny lie in the tall grass for a moment trying to recover, before regaining its senses and bounding off to safety.

Billy turned to face Henry, a look of hatred on his face. It was as if he was looking past Henry to a place beyond him, like he didn't see Henry at all. He took a slow step forward and Henry retreated a step in return.

"You always gotta interfere. No different than when you came between me and Jack!" he growled, taking another step forward.

Henry took another step back. The scared look on his face was completely lost on Billy. He didn't see Henry; he only saw someone that was standing in his way.

Henry had reached the edge of the cliff and he looked over his shoulder to the bottom of the quarry, far below. Billy had closed the distance between them and was standing an arm's length away. His eyes looked glassy, unseeing, unknowing.

"Billy! Billy don't!" he screamed.

Billy reached out his right hand and pushed Henry on the shoulder. It was just enough that he lost his balance and his right foot slid on the rocks lining the edge of the cliff. He fell on one knee with his left foot hanging in mid-air. He had time enough to look up at Billy and then the edge of the cliff gave way, and he was sent sprawling through the air, down and away from Billy. His arms flailed, trying to grab hold of something that wasn't there. He landed on the quarry floor, far below, with a loud thud. A large plume of dust spread into the sky above him. Billy looked over the edge to where his kid brother had just fallen. Henry was obscured by the dust cloud from below. Billy didn't wait for it to settle. The veil had been lifted from his eyes and he was seeing clearly now. Billy scrambled down the cliff to where his brother lie. Henry was still alive, but he had a scared look on his face and he wasn't moving.

"Oh my God, Henry are you okay?" Billy said, tears streaming down his face.

Billy knew the answer to his question before he asked it. He was hoping that somehow this could all turn out, but he knew deep down in the pit of his stomach, that Henry was not okay.

Henry stared straight ahead, his throat moved up and down as if he would speak, but only gurgling sounds came from him. There was blood streaming from his ears and nostrils and his skin was grey and clammy. He tried to speak but only blood frothed at his lips. Billy held his hand tightly and tears fell on Henry's face as he bent over him. Billy wiped his tears from his kid brother's face.

"I'm sorry Henry, so sorry. I'd change places with you, if only I could. I swear I would. You're the good one. I'm the one that's no good. I'm the one that deserves to die!" Billy blurted out.

Henry took as deep a breath as he could muster and managed to whisper.

"It's okay Billy, I get to see Mom now," Henry said quietly, exhaled and then remained still.

His eyes were fixed on Billy's, but they were sightless eyes, he had gone to be with his Mom, as he had said. Billy closed Henry's eyes and gathered him in his arms and cried. He held him and talked to him for over an hour, until he ran out of things to say. He apologized again and again, and he prayed to God to protect Henry and watch over him. He was supposed to watch out for his kid brother. What had he done?

Billy couldn't bring himself to let go of Henry. He knew that it was dumb, but he didn't want to leave him here all alone, so he stayed, and held him tightly, waiting for someone to find them.

CHAPTER EIGHT

Billy stayed that way for three agonizing hours, until some other kids trying to escape the heat of the day, happened upon them. Billy called for them to help, but they didn't hear him. He was parched from sitting in the sun for hours and his lips were dry. All he managed was a soft croak of a call. He waved with his left hand until they noticed him, and came over, hesitantly. Two young girls and a boy, wearing nothing but their bathing suits came over, slowly.

"Everything okay?" the boy asked carefully.

But, before Billy could answer him, the girls who were standing just a few steps further back, gasped loudly and covered their mouths with their hands. They took a couple of steps backward, but the boy remained.

"Is he okay? He's okay, right?" he asked nervously, craning his neck to look around Billy, without moving his feet.

"Can you run and call for an ambulance please, right away, as quickly as you can?" Billy said, fighting back the tears that flowed freely anyway.

Billy knew there was no urgency. It was too late for Henry, but even though it made no sense, he still didn't want Henry to have to wait for help.

"Sure, you bet. He'll be fine, you'll see. My Mom's a nurse at the hospital and they'll take good care of him there," he said.

"Hurry!" Billy yelled.

The boy turned and ran toward the cliff, without saying another word, and the girls were fast on his heels. They scrambled up the trail, to the top, and out of sight.

It was just him and Henry once again, same as always, that part hadn't changed. It had always been just Henry and him against the world. Only now, that had all changed. From now on it would be just Billy against the world. It made him shiver just thinking about it and he held his brother closer. Henry was cool to the touch now. Billy could close his eyes, hold his brother tightly and make himself believe that his brother wasn't dead before, but he couldn't any longer. Henry was growing colder, there was no denying, that he wasn't just sleeping in his arms, waiting for help. This realization brought with it a new bout of sadness, that had him sobbing and talking to Henry again.

Minutes seemed to take hours and Billy was okay with that. He knew that once help came, he would have to let go of his kid brother and he couldn't bear the thought of it, the finality of it.

He could hear the wail of sirens in the distance now and he hated the sound of them. They were coming to take Henry away from him. He needed to be with him, but he knew that he was running out of time. If only he could go back and change the events of this afternoon, then he would gladly do it. He would change spots with him in a heartbeat, but sadly that wasn't the case. He would have a lifetime of regret, for what he had done.

The sirens were getting louder and Billy could now see the lights over the crest of the quarry's cliff.

"They're almost here Henry. Hang in there, little brother," Billy said, sobbing.

Tears ran in streams down his face leaving dirty trails on his and Henry's dusty faces. Billy wiped at the tears on Henry's face but he only made it worse, now there were swirls of dirt on his cheeks.

"I'm sorry Henry, for crying on you, for being a shitty big brother and most of all I'm sorry that I'm still alive and you aren't."

Billy looked to the top of the quarry and saw a couple of police cars, an ambulance and a fire truck, all sitting there with their lights flashing. A group of kids on bikes had gathered there as well, trying to get a look at what was happening, far below. There was also an older gentleman wearing a blue fedora, who looked completely out of place, given the circumstances. He lingered for a few moments and then continued on his way. One of the policemen was doing his best to keep the kids back from the edge and before long he had marked off the spot with yellow police tape.

Two paramedics made their way gingerly down the slope, carrying a stretcher. The woman paramedic approached Billy while the man stood by her side. She could tell with one look that there was no need for urgency. Henry's blood had dried to a dark red, almost black. There were streams of it from each nostril and each ear and Billy's forearms and hands were covered with it. Henry's face was ghostly white and his mouth was slightly open.

The woman touched Billy on the shoulder and he flinched as though he'd been caught by surprise, even though he could see her coming, the entire time.

"My name is Abril and this is my partner Dave. We need to take a look at your brother here. Is he your brother?" she asked.

Billy clutched Henry tighter to him and held him slightly away from her.

"I know this is hard, but we have to. Can we have a look at him?" she said, softly.

Billy set Henry back down on his legs and straightened his back. It was as far as he was willing to go. He wasn't leaving him. Abril knelt beside the two brothers and got to work examining Henry. She understood that Billy wasn't moving and that she would have to check him while he was on Billy's lap.

She took his pulse, opened one of his eyes and shone a flash light in it and then looked up at her partner and shook her head grimly. She looked in his ears, nose and mouth and examined him quickly for broken bones. Then she patted him on the chest gently and then looked up at Billy.

"I'm sorry, very sorry, but we are going to have to move him now. You can ride with us to the hospital if you would like, but we do have to leave," she said, and motioned to Dave to bring the stretcher.

"Is there someone we can call to meet us at the hospital, your Mom, Dad?" Abril asked.

"My Dad, I guess," Billy said, reluctantly.

"Okay when we get to the ambulance, Dave will make the call for you, okay?" she said.

Billy gave Henry one last hug, placed him gently on the ground and stood up slowly. His back and legs ached from sitting for so long. He bent backward to stretch his lower back and when he was done, Abril and Dave had finished putting Henry on the stretcher.

"You go on ahead, Dave and I will follow you up," Abril said.

Billy wasn't having any of it. He plodded alongside them, on their slow climb up the quarry face.

They loaded Henry into the back of the ambulance. There was a small crowd of kids gathered on the other side of the police tape. Billy saw them but he didn't bother to look at who they were, it didn't matter in the least. The only thing that mattered to him right now, was Henry.

"Hello Billy, I'm sorry, but before you get in the ambulance I need to ask you a few questions. I need to know what happened here. Just tell me in your own words, and then I'll let you go, okay?" Officer Gamble said.

"I've already called his Father; he'll meet us at the hospital," Officer Gamble said to Abril and then turned back towards Billy.

"Okay, that's good," Abril said, from behind them.

Billy stood looking at the ground. He was tired, his legs and back ached and his head hurt most of all. He didn't feel like talking but he just wanted to get this part over with, so that he could be with Henry again.

"Henry and I came to go swimming, because it was such a hot day, you know? I found a little bunny in the tall grass over there," Billy said, pointing to the tall grass by the edge of the cliff.

"I picked him up by the neck so that he wouldn't bite me. Henry was scared that I would hurt him so he was hitting at my arms for me to drop him. I let go of the bunny and shoved Henry. He lost his balance and fell," Billy concluded, still looking at the ground.

"I see, okay, you can go. We'll talk later," Officer Gamble said.

Billy climbed into the ambulance and sat with Henry. There was a blanket covering him. Billy removed it from atop Henry's face and then laid his head on Henry's chest. He rode that way, until they got to the hospital.

Their Dad was there when they arrived. Abril and Dave explained to him what had happened. He was distraught of course, but he never comforted Billy.

"What the Hell happened? You were supposed to look after him. He relied on you, and you let him down. I can't even look at you right now," Bill said to Billy, and then walked away.

Billy was okay with that, he deserved it.

They went through the formality of pronouncing Henry dead and then Billy and his Dad went home. Not a word was spoken the entire car ride. His Dad barely spoke to him at all in the next few weeks, as a matter of fact. They both grieved in their own way.

Billy's Dad drank more than ever and he was rarely home. Billy kept to himself. He was tired again all the time. The black circles reappeared under his eyes and he was nearly always in a foul mood.

He missed Henry more than anything. It hurt so bad, that he didn't know if he could continue on. His new addiction had been pushed aside for the time being. Even that fat kid Jack, who had grown considerably in the last few months, didn't interest him. He couldn't bring himself to torment him, or anyone or anything for that matter. It was partly because he was just too depressed to care and partly because he knew that Henry wouldn't want him to.

He continued that way for months after Henry's death and funeral. The police ruled Henry's death an accident and never bothered him again. He rarely saw his Dad anymore and if he did they never spoke anyway. He went to school but he didn't hear what the teachers said. Henry had been his only true friend as it turned out, and now he was completely alone.

He decided, much as his Father had, years before, that he needed a change of scenery. But, before he left he was going to see that fat kid Jack. That was when it all started. If it weren't for him, then Henry would still be alive. He had convinced himself somehow that it was Jack's fault that Henry was dead, and he intended to make him pay for that. He also thought that killing him would get him out of the funk that he was in. What better way, than to kill the person that killed his brother.

Billy waited for him by the same bridge that he had first tormented him. How fitting it would be, to go back to where it all started.

He sat on top of the same railing as he had, many months before.

"You know, it's your fault that Henry's dead," Billy said quietly, as he jumped down from the railing.

Jack just kept walking without saying a word.

Billy stood in the middle of the path with his eyes cast to the ground. He stood in much the same manner as Henry had done on several occasions. Aside from the family resemblance however, Billy and henry were nothing alike. Henry was kind and gentle, a good soul. Billy was nasty and mean, and he was here to exact some revenge.

"It should have been you that was killed. I would have enjoyed that. I hate it when people make me do things I don't want to do. I like doing things because I want to do them. It's better that way. It feels better. It fills me up," he said, still looking at the ground.

Jack stopped walking and stood in the middle of the path, about ten yards away.

Billy stood looking at the ground and began to cry. He wiped one eye with the back of his hand and then the other, sniffling as he did. Eventually he fell to his knees and began to sob.

Jack stood motionless. He wasn't sure what to do, but after several seconds he started walking again. Billy began to speak again, louder this time.

"Usually it fills me up," he began.

Jack stopped again, with a stupid, confused look on his face.

"I thought it would fill me up. It's the first time that it didn't. I have an idea why it didn't. Pretty sure, anyhow. I'm still learning, but I'm willing to practice until I get it right," Billy said, looking up for the first time, an evil grin spreading across his face.

"Well, have fun with that," Jack said, and started to move past him.

"How dare you talk to me that way, you fat fuck? Who do you think you are?" Billy screamed.

He jumped from his knees with all the agility of a cat, and was behind Jack, with his arm wrapped around his neck, before he knew what had happened. He held the point of his knife to Jack's throat.

"This is for Henry, and you're going to help fill me up, while we're at it. We'll have to go further into the woods, because it's going to take a while," Billy said, flashing his sadistic grin once again.

Billy was feeling better already. He could feel Jack's heart rate increase, along with his adrenaline.

He pushed Jack in front of him, down a smaller path and into the woods. Jack turned to plead with him, and that just served, to fill him up more. He threw his head back and laughed with delight, that warm, inviting feeling, rushing in.

Billy stopped laughing and the warm feeling was replaced with shock and horror. Jack drove his right foot as hard as he could, up between Billy's legs. He fell over on his side, writhing in pain.

"That was for Henry sure enough, and this is for me," Jack said, as he kicked him hard in the side of the face.

The world swayed, went out of focus, and then black.

Billy's knife fell from his limp hand and Jack reached down to pick it up. He stood over him for a moment, looking down at him.

Jack smiled at Billy laying there unconscious and then a frown slowly replaced it.

"What made you the way that you are, Billy Johnson? What happened to you to make you so unhappy, so evil? I can forgive what you have done to me, but what you did to your brother, is unforgiveable," he said.

Jack knelt beside him and checked that he was breathing. Billy stirred a little as he did. Jack stood up and threw the knife into the woods as far as he could, turned and continued down the small path, out to the main one and across the bridge.

CHAPTER NINE

The side of Billy's face hurt like hell, from where that bastard Jack had kicked him. He had completely taken him by surprise. He had better learn to be a little more careful and not to be so arrogant. If he ever ran into Jack again he'd be sorry, that was for sure, but in the meantime he had different plans.

The incident with Jack served to strengthen his resolve, to get the hell out of town. There was no one that would even notice that he was gone. He wondered just how long it would take, before his Dad would even know, that he had left.

He was old enough to be on his own anyway. He was just a couple of months shy of his sixteenth birthday. He wasn't big for his age but he could grow a full beard if he wanted to and could probably pass himself off as eighteen. He would likely have to, if he wanted to get himself a job, but then again, summer was nearly upon them and he could probably find seasonal work.

He had no plan as to where he would go, or what he would do. All he knew was that he had to get out of there. Like his Father before him, he just knew that he had to run from the memories that haunted him.

He headed west and kept running from the memories, until he ran out of real estate. He found himself on the west coast, far away from home.

Unlike his Dad, who drank to dull the pain that he felt, Billy had another vice. His was far worse than his Dad's, ever could have been. Yes, it's true that his Dad's drinking had had a very negative affect on him and Henry. There was no arguing that point, but Billy's vice was far worse.

At first, Billy was excited to travel, see and experience new things that his small town hadn't offered him. He found that there were hours and almost days that would go by, without him thinking about his kid brother. He was almost happy. He found that he didn't need filling up. The adventure itself was enough. For the most part, he didn't feel that hollow feeling inside.

There were times that he thought of Henry and it made him sad, and like his Dad, he would drink until the pain subsided. There were times when the hollow feeling would start to grow again, but there was always some new adventure to begin, that would temporarily take his mind away from it.

Billy got a job for the summer clearing a farmer's fields of rocks and trees. It was an old dairy farm with two hundred acres, that the farmer now grew corn and soybeans on. He raised chickens to sell in town along with their eggs and he also raised cattle and pigs which he sold in town as well. It was hard work and he was exhausted at the end of the day, but it didn't allow for much idle time or idle thoughts. The entire farm was in dis-array. Billy spent weeks giving the barn and out buildings a fresh coat of red paint with white trim. The wire fence that ran the perimeter of the farm also needed tending to. He cleared trees from around the pond, and on the really warm days he would sneak off for a dip. The summer passed quickly and the farmer didn't need his services any longer. He hooked him up with a friend of his that needed a good lad such as Billy, to shovel snow for the winter. Billy was happy to do it, he liked working outdoors. All the hard work had made him strong and he felt better than he could ever remember. That is of course, if you don't count how he felt, after he filled himself up. That was okay, because he hardly missed it. He thought that he could probably go on this way, without ever needing to fill himself up again.

·   ·   ·   ·   ·

Billy stayed at the farmer's house that he had worked for in the summer and he took on-line classes to finish high school. The farmer took him into town every morning to go to work and he picked him up every night. He was as nice an old man as you would ever meet. His wife had died nearly four years earlier and his kids were older, and had moved away.

"I can't tell you how happy I am, that God saw fit to drop you on my doorstep. I was a lonely old coot before you got here," Jacob said.

"I'm not so sure that it was God that brought me to the farm, but I'm glad to be here, all the same."

"I believe that everything happens for a reason."

"So, why do you think that I'm here?"

"That we both needed to heal. There was a hole in our lives, that had to be filled. These last few months have been the happiest, since Margaret died. Thank you for that."

Billy didn't respond, he thought that Jacob was great, but he was always waiting for the other shoe to drop. He had trouble, letting go of the past and believing that this was real.

. . . . .

Billy took a liking to him right away but he needed time to trust him. None of this happened overnight. It was a process that took many months, and It was so gradual that Billy didn't even realize it was happening. He filled the role that his Father never could, and after a while he became more like a Father to him than his own Dad had ever been. Jacob came to think of Billy as one of his own sons.

"I'm not sure what brought you here, Billy and I don't need to know. Maybe someday you'll trust me enough to tell me, but until then, I'm okay not knowing. Sometimes I see the sadness in your eyes and it troubles me. That's all."

"Someday," Billy said, lost in thought.

Billy didn't like to think about Henry let alone talk about him. Henry and he did share many good memories but he couldn't think of him without feeling guilty and terribly sad. Those thoughts and feelings were a slippery slope back to his past. It was easier to just avoid thinking about it all together.

"My brother died, like Margaret," Billy blurted out.

"I see," he said, and left it that.

Jacob could identify with the pain that Billy was living with. He missed his wife so much sometimes, he wished he were dead. Billy helped with that. He had someone that depended on him and that gave his life meaning once again. Billy felt the same way. It had always been Billy and Henry against the world and now he was alone. The farmer filled that void in Billy's life as well.

It wasn't a matter of misery loving company. No, they were truly happy to have each other in their lives and they both prospered from the relationship that they forged together.

Jacob, would tell many stories about his beloved wife Margaret.

"My guess is that you're too young to understand, but she was my whole world, Billy. She was the first person, the only person that I wanted to see every morning when I awoke, and the last person that I saw every night when I went to sleep. She made me a better, kinder version of myself. Oh, sometimes I would argue that I knew better, when she tried to tell me something, but the truth is she always knew what was best. If you ever find someone to love like that, hold on to her, with everything you have and don't let go," Jacob said, smiling sadly.

"I can tell that you loved her very much. I can hear it your voice, every time you talk about her. I can even tell when you are thinking about her. It's written all over your face."

"I'm a lucky man, Billy. To be blessed with the love of such a good woman. Well…let's just say, that it's more than I could have ever hoped for."

It turns out that Margaret was his favourite topic in the whole world, and after not too long a time, Billy felt as though he had known the woman himself, and he had to say, he liked her very much.

"What about your family Billy? You don't talk about them much?"

"Not much to say, I guess. Some day I'll tell you… maybe," Billy said.

As time went on and Billy felt more and more comfortable with Jacob, he began to open up. Jacob encouraged him. He could see how passionately Jacob talked about his beloved Margaret and how therapeutic it had become. He wondered if it could be the same for him.

He started slowly, hesitantly. He didn't like talking about Henry, it felt like he was betraying him somehow. The more he talked about Henry the easier it got and the easier it became to remember the good times and try to forget the bad stuff. Jacob was delighted to see how Billy was enjoying talking about Henry. He knew it would be good for him to talk about his brother, in much the same way that it was good for him, to talk about Margaret.

"Henry sounds like he was a great kid. I know you love him, and I can tell, you miss him a lot, talking about him, helps to keep him with you," Jacob said.

"I know. He was a great kid, far better than me. I miss him so much sometimes, I can't stand it."

"It gets easier with time. Time heals all wounds. You know, you were a little rough around the edges when you got here, but I think those edges have softened a lot. I believe you and Henry are more alike than you give yourself

THE SUFFERING

credit for," Jacob said.

Jacob was wrong, this was one wound that didn't hurt as much as time went by, but it never did heal.

"Thanks for getting me to talk about Henry, it really does help," Billy said.

Jacob reached over and put his large hand on top of Billy's.

"You're welcome son. That's what we do for our loved ones. We support them in good times and in bad," Jacob said.

Billy took his other hand and placed it on top of Jacob's.

"I love you," Billy said, in his head, but he wasn't quite ready to say it aloud.

"I couldn't love you any more if you were my own flesh and blood," Jacob said, wiping tears from his eyes.

"Well that's not true, I guess. My own miserable kids never come and visit their old man any more. So, I guess it's just you and me against the world kid," Jacob said.

Billy broke down and cried. Jacob had no way of knowing, that was what Billy used to say to his kid brother. Jacob hugged Billy tightly and he continued to cry, but now they were tears of happiness. Billy had never been so happy in his entire life. He felt loved and he felt whole for the first time. He had the Father that he had always wanted, that Henry and him always wanted. Oh, how he wished that Henry was here, to enjoy the moment with him.

Over the next two years, Jacob and Billy became closer and closer. Billy began to call him Dad and he loved the way it sounded. Jacob, for his part, loved the way it sounded too. Billy wondered how Jacob's children couldn't see how amazing a man their Father was and Jacob couldn't believe that Billy's Father didn't see what an amazing son he had.

Whatever the reasons, they were just happy that circumstances had brought them together.

On Billy's birthday Jacob surprised him with a new truck. It was an older truck, but it was new to him and it was in perfect shape.

"Now, I have one condition. When it comes time for you to go work in town in the fall, I still want to drive you. I look forward to the time we spend and the conversations that we have on those trips," Jacob said.

"I wouldn't have it any other way. Thanks, Dad, I love you," Billy said.

"My pleasure son. Now maybe you can meet some nice little thing from town, instead of being stuck out here on the farm, with me all of the time."

"I don't mind; I love it here," Billy said.

"I know, but a young man needs to be with people of his own age, from time to time," Jacob said.

Billy hadn't considered that before. He was perfectly happy hanging out with his Dad. Truth be told, he never had any friends growing up, and he never had a steady girlfriend either.

There was this one girl, Jill. He messed around with her behind the bleachers a couple of times, but then he went through one of his hollow spells and he stopped seeing her. After that, the other girls at school looked at him differently. Girls talk, and Jill had a lot to say about Billy, and none of it was very nice. It didn't matter, he was too pre-occupied with other things at the time, to pay it much notice.

That seemed a life time ago, like it was someone else's life. This was Billy now and he was happy to just work and hang out with Jacob. He didn't need any more than that.

He was so proud of his new truck and he was happy to run into town to get things, whenever his Dad needed him to. Jacob taught him how to drive on the farm and he learned quickly. He never actually got his driver's license but around these parts, no one seemed to care if he did or not.

Everyone in town liked Billy. He was always smiling and always helpful. They could all see why Jacob had taken a liking to him. They all knew a Billy that was far different from the one that Jack and Henry knew.

The hollowness that had had a grip on him, seemed to be a thing of the past and that was a relief for Billy. He never liked hurting animals or people. Well, he did get a bit of a charge out of tormenting kids from time to time, but he never enjoyed, actually hurting them. The hollowness made him do things that he never would have done otherwise. He was just glad that that part of his life was over and that he could make a fresh start. Of course, he wished that Henry was here to enjoy it with him. Henry would have loved Jacob and he knew that Jacob would have adored Henry. What wasn't to like? Henry was the sweetest, gentlest kid, that you would ever meet.

Jacob had one son and one daughter born two years apart. They lived in the city. They thought that they were too good to live the simple life of a farmer. Jacob said that they got that from their Mother. He wasn't putting her down, he would never talk poorly of his beloved Margaret. He just meant that she originally came from the city and she never truly loved the country like he did. She loved him more than anything and so she stayed, but she was still a city girl at heart.

Jacobs's daughter Abby was thirty-five and she had a boy and a girl. His son, Frank was thirty-seven and had a boy and a girl of his own. Jacob used to see his kids and grandkids on every holiday and they would sometimes spend a couple of weeks on the farm in the summer. After Margaret died, their visits continued for a while, but slowly over time, their visits became further and further apart. Margaret was the glue that held the family together and once she was gone, they seemed to grow apart.

Now, Jacob very rarely saw them anymore. They were always too busy to come and see him. Billy could hear the sadness in his voice, when he talked about not seeing his kids and grandkids.

"No matter. God has seen fit to send you my way, and I'm thankful for that," Jacob said.

"You know, I'm not too sure how I feel about God. We've had our differences over the years," Billy said.

"That's what makes God so wonderful. He'll be waiting to take you back, whenever you decide that you want Him in your life again," Jacob said.

"I'll have to think about it," Billy said.

Jacob didn't pressure him; he just let it be. He hoped that Billy would find God again but in the meantime, he prayed for him all the same.

"I can tell that it makes you sad when you talk about your kids and grandkids. We have a few days to spare. Everything is caught up around here. We could drive into the city and visit them if you'd like."

Billy liked the idea of going on a small road trip with his Dad and he liked the idea of driving his truck even more.

"If we were going to do that, we should call before we go. They might be busy and I wouldn't want to impose," Jacob said.

"I think it's better if we don't, just surprise them. That way they can't say no."

"You know what? That's a great idea. I think we should go. We can leave first thing in the morning, that should get us there by the time they're home from work," Jacob said.

Later in the day, Billy found Jacob milling about the barn. He was cleaning up things that he had already tended to. Billy watched from a distance as he sat on a stool and whittled a stick for a while. Then he checked on the animals, went back to whittling and then checked on the animals again.

"You nervous about tomorrow?" Billy asked.

Jacob jumped at the sound of his voice. "I won't see tomorrow, if you sneak up on me like that again," he said, grabbing at his chest and laughing.

"I didn't sneak up on you. Looks like you have something on your mind, and I think I know what it is."

"You're right. I did the best for my family that I could. Hindsight being twenty-twenty and all, you know? I guess I could have done better," Jacob said, sadly.

"Don't beat yourself up about it. You're still trying, aren't you?"

"I guess you're right. I just want things to go well tomorrow."

The next morning, he was up before his alarm, made breakfast and had it on the table before Billy was awake.

"Come on sleepy head. Breakfast is going to get cold. Time to get up."

Billy wasn't in the habit of sleeping in, so he was confused when he awoke. He looked at the clock on his night stand and he understood. The display read 5:45 A.M. He hadn't slept in at all, Jacob was just in a hurry to get going, and he couldn't be idle any longer.

"Coming," Billy said.

He got dressed and went into the kitchen. Jacob had prepared a spread of food that was surely enough for six full grown men. Billy laughed at the sight of it. There was a stack of French toast, pancakes, bacon, sausage, scrambled eggs, toast and a large plate of cut up oranges.

"Too much? I just couldn't sit still. I'm just nervous I guess," Jacob said, sounding a little embarrassed.

"No need to explain. This is a big deal for you, I get it."

Jacob had already eaten and he paced back and forth in the kitchen, waiting for Billy to finish. When Billy emptied his plate, Jacob was there to snatch it away from him and wash it in the sink. Jacob was relieved, when he had finished.

They hit the road and Jacob never stopped talking and moving the entire trip. He squirmed in his seat, and drummed his fingers on the arm rest. Billy looked over at Jacob and smiled.

"I know, I know. I just can't sit still."

"You're like a little kid on Christmas morning.

"Maybe we should have called ahead."

"And, maybe I should have given you a sedative," Billy said, and they shared a laugh.

Jacob told stories about his kids the entire trip. Billy could hear the love in his words and in his voice. He wondered how people could turn their backs on their families, like his own Father had on him, or like Jacob's children had. How could they not see, how wonderful and loving a man their Father was? Billy enjoyed listening to Jacob's stories. It was a good thing because he could hardly get a word in, the entire trip, but It did seem to help him stop fidgeting.

The time flew by, and before they knew it, the five-hour trip was behind them and they pulled up, out front of Abby's house.

·　　·　　·　　·　　·

Jacob walked up to the front door and Billy hung back a bit.

"Are you coming?"

"Yeah…it's just," Billy said, hesitating.

"Now listen, Billy. You're as much, one of my kids as Abby and Frank. I don't want you to ever doubt that."

"I know. I don't want to give you the wrong impression. I'm a little concerned what they might think of me, that's all."

"Don't give it another thought. I have your back," he said, putting his arm around him and giving him a hug.

Abby answered the door, and was of course surprised to see her Father standing there.

"Dad, what are you doing here?" she asked.

Not, oh my God, Dad what are you doing here? It's so good to see you. Just, what are you doing here? Billy's heart sank, he was hoping for a better response.

"I thought I'd surprise you with a visit. So, here I am, Surprise!" Jacob said.

"You should have called before driving all the way out here. We're always so busy during the week," she said.

Abby stood, holding the door open, but she still hadn't invited them in.

"I guess you're right, I probably should have, but then you would have told me how busy you were, and then another week, another month, another year would go by, and I still wouldn't see you," Jacob said.

"Oh Dad, that's not true," she said.

"Can we come in?" Jacob asked.

Abby hadn't even looked at Billy yet, but now she seemed to notice him for the first time. She looked him up and down, trying to figure out how he fit into the picture.

"Abby, this is Billy. He's been helping me around the farm and I've become quite attached to him," he said, clapping him on the shoulder.

Billy reached out his hand to shake hers. Abby turned and walked away.

"Yes, come in," she said.

Once they were in, they went and sat in the living room. Jacob introduced Billy to Abby's husband and the kids.

"Could you call Frank and ask him to come over as well, please?" Jacob asked.

"I'm sure that he's busy, but I'll call."

She pulled out her cell phone and called. "Hi, Frank. Dad's here, and he has some guy with him. Anyway, he wants you to come over, to visit. I know, I told him that you would be busy. Okay. I'll tell him," she said.

"He said, that he won't be able to stay long, but he'll come over."

"Thanks. Now where did my grandkids get to? I'd like to see them," Jacob said.

"They have homework, Dad. That's what happens when you show up unannounced like this," Abby said.

"A few minutes wouldn't hurt," Jacob said.

"Maybe later," she said curtly.

Billy tried to smile and be the good son, but he hated the way Abby treated Jacob. He felt uncomfortable being there and it showed. He crossed his legs but soon became uncomfortable, so he sat with his hands on his knees, picking at his callouses.

"He isn't slow, is he?" Abby asked in a hushed voice, looking at Billy.

"Abby! That's a terrible thing to say. No!" Jacob said, loudly.

"What? I was just curious."

Billy could feel his cheeks flash red, but it wasn't from embarrassment. He kept his cool for Jacob's sake, but he wanted to strangle her. He took a couple of deep breaths to calm himself and then tried his best to ignore her, for the duration of the visit. Frank and his family showed up shortly after, and it was a welcome distraction.

"Good to see you Frank, and the rest of you as well," Jacob said to his family. He shook Frank's hand and the rest of them brushed past him, and went to sit on the couch. It wasn't long before his children, disappeared as well.

"This is Billy. He's been helping me around the farm, and we've been getting along quite well," he said, smiling at Billy.

"Nice to meet you, Billy," Frank said, shaking his hand.

"So, why the visit, out of the blue?" Frank asked.

"I don't see you guys much any more, since your Mother passed. I miss you, and I never get to see my grandchildren any more," Jacob said.

"We just saw you a few months ago. We're very busy, you know, can't just drop everything and run out to the farm. That's another thing; why don't you just sell the farm and move closer, if you want to see us more? Sometimes, I think that you love that damn farm, more than us," Abby said.

Jacob didn't respond. He just smiled sadly. The conversation continued, but it was strained at best, after that. Jacob tried, but eventually he had run out of things to say.

"Well, I've taken up enough of your time. We have a long ride back and we should be going."

"I don't know what you thought. Next time, let us know that you're coming, and we'll try to make some time," Abby said.

"It was nice to see them, thanks for coming with me Billy," Jacob said, when they got back to the truck.

"No problem, I know how much it meant to you."

"Yes, and now that I have, I'm okay for a while. I always want things to be like they were, hope that they will be, you know? It just hasn't been the same since Margaret died and it's clear that it never will. I guess I'm just tired of trying to force something that isn't there," Jacob said.

Billy didn't say anything, neither of them did, for nearly an hour. Jacob sat looking out the window. Billy wasn't sure, but it sounded like he was crying. His heart went out to him, but he let him be, to sort through things for a while.

Finally, Jacob broke the silence. "Thanks for coming Billy, it meant the world to me."

"Of course, I'd do anything for you."

"I know, you're a good boy, not like those other two, we just went to see," he said, reached over and rubbed Billy's shoulder.

Jacob seemed happier after that. It was as though he decided to forget about that for a while, and just be happy in the moment. Billy found that it was an admirable trait to possess. He wasn't able, to just shut things off like that. The old Billy would have liked very much to go and hurt Abby and to a lesser extent, Frank, but this version of Billy, just let it go, because Jacob did.

The conversation changed and they never spoke of Abby or Frank, for the rest of the trip.

The weeks after their trip to the city seemed better for Jacob. For a while leading up to their trip, he seemed restless, but now he seemed more at ease.

"You seem different since our trip into the city," Billy said.

"It's like I said before. From time to time, I get to missing my kids and want to reach out to them and then when I do, I am reminded why I really don't like them all that much. I guess you can't really pick your family, present company excluded, of course," he said, pausing to think.

"I guess that really didn't answer to what you just said, did it? I get to thinking about what things would be like and how they could be better, or how I could change things. When you start thinking like that, then you start missing the things that are right in front of you. The things that already make you happy and that you should be grateful for. I have a lot to be thankful for and it's time for me to get back to realizing that. So, I guess it's just the way that you look at things sometimes, that can make all the difference in the world. If you think that you should be happy, you will be, and if you think that you should be miserable, then you will be. Pretty straight forward stuff, I think," Jacob said.

"That makes a lot of sense to me. You always have a way of making everything seem so easy. I wish I could be more like that," Billy said.

"Stick with me kid, I'm bound to wear off on you eventually. Don't forget, I'm an old man. I didn't start out this way, I've mellowed a lot over the years. A lot of things that seemed to matter when I was a young man, don't seem to carry the same weight, now that I'm older," he said.

Billy appreciated the conversations that he had with Jacob. He never had anyone older to talk to, while he was growing up. He pretended that he had things all figured out for Henry's sake, but the truth of the matter was, that he was scared and unsure a lot of the time. It was nice now that he could sit back and listen to Jacob's stories and learn something from them.

"I really enjoy listening to your stories, I never had that as a kid. I appreciate you taking the time."

"It's my pleasure, son. People around these parts are probably sick of the same old stories, so it's nice to have some new blood around. Someday you'll probably get sick of my stories too, but until that day comes, I'll probably continue to talk your ear off, any chance I get," Jacob said, smiling warmly.

"That's not likely to happen," Billy said, and gave Jacob a nice big hug.

CHAPTER TEN

Billy felt loved and he was in the best frame of mind of his young life. He appreciated the fortunate turn of events, that had brought him into Jacob's life.

Billy was so into the moment, remembering all the good times that he had spent with Jacob that for a short while, at least, he had forgotten about his present predicament. The sun was now high in the sky, but soon it would be descending, on its way to the darkness. That thought didn't scare him like it did, on the previous night. He was starting to come to grips with the fact, that he might not leave this mountain alive. He still wanted to live, but he was starting to make peace with the fact, that he might not. He wondered if this was the beginning of the end, for Billy Johnson. Was this the defining moment that took him from struggling to stay alive, to being okay with death? No, he still wanted to live and he still had some things to work through, before he was ready to call it.

He had a lot of regrets. That was an understatement. He felt as though he had let Jacob down. Not while he was alive, but after his death. He felt as though he tarnished his memory by what he had done. Even now, it all seemed like some sort of bad dream. Jacob had talked about how Margaret had made him a better person, and he knew exactly what he meant. Henry had tried to fill that role, but he wouldn't let him. Jacob certainly had, partly because he was such a kind soul and partly because Billy was ready to let someone in.

CHAPTER ELEVEN

Three days after Billy and Jacob went to the city to visit his kids, Jacob sat with him on the front stoop of the farm house. Jacob was unnaturally fidgety and he was quieter than normal. Billy could tell that there was something weighing on his mind.

"You know I think of you as my son?" he finally said, and paused for a moment.

"And I think of you as my Dad. So, what's up? I can tell that there's something on your mind. Does it have something to do with our visit the other day?" Billy asked.

"It has everything to do with our little visit to the city, as a matter of fact. I got to thinking afterwards. Neither of my kids could care a less for this old farm, or for me as it turns out. They're happy with their lives in the city and they have no use for me or the farm. I believe that I won't be around too much longer. It's just a feeling I get, I can't really explain it. They say that some people just know when it's their time. Anyway, I've made an appointment with my lawyer for tomorrow to change my will. I would like to leave the farm to you Billy. In fact, nothing would please me more," he said smiling, a content look on his face.

"I don't know what to say, other than, it doesn't matter because you're not going anywhere. You're going to be sick of me, because we are going to be spending so much time together, for years to come."

"I hope you're right, but sadly I don't think so," Jacob said.

"Why? Have you been feeling alright?" Billy asked, panic creeping into his voice.

"No, no, nothing like that. I feel fit as a fiddle. I might be way off base, but it just feels like my time. I can't explain it. I shouldn't have said anything about it, I'm sorry, I didn't mean to alarm you," Jacob said, smiling wanly.

They sat in silence for a few minutes before Billy spoke again.

"I would be honoured to look after the farm for you, after you're gone; you know, many years down the road."

Jacob laughed, "Okay, many years from now."

"I'm glad we talked. I know you will do me proud Billy, when the time comes. Now give me a hug, I'm going to go lie down for a nap."

Billy hugged Jacob and then watched him walk down the hall and into his bedroom. He continued to sit on the porch for quite some time, playing their conversation over in his mind. Firstly, he couldn't imagine his life without Jacob in it. Secondly, he was blown away that he would leave him the farm. He would make very sure that Jacob's trust in him was repaid by looking after it, as best he could.

Billy didn't believe that Jacob could foretell his own death, but on some level, he was worried all the same. He thought that he would go check on him just to be sure. He crept slowly down the hall and quietly entered his room. He was as quiet as he could possibly be, partly because he didn't want to disturb him and partly because he felt stupid. He knew it was childish to think that Jacob was anything other, than just fine.

Billy stood at the foot of his bed and watched for the rise and fall of his covers. It had to be the darkness playing tricks on his eyes, because he didn't see any perceptible movement. He listened intently for the telltale sound of Jacob breathing loudly, while he slept. Billy strained to hear but heard nothing. He moved nearer and still nothing. He was starting to get worried, so he moved closer, but still no movement or sound came from beneath the covers. Billy reached out with his right hand to touch Jacob's shoulder, but before he could, Jacob re-positioned himself in bed, letting out a loud groan as he did.

Billy had to cover his mouth for fear of making a sound. His heart rate had doubled in an instant, it scared him so badly. He left the room quietly and went out into the hall, where he laughed a little to himself, took a calming breath and continued with his day. Jacob had almost convinced him, that he just might know that he was going to die. Billy knew that it was preposterous, but he still had him scared all the same.

Billy put those thoughts out of his mind and went out to the barn to do some chores, before starting on supper. Hard work and Billy were certainly no strangers and he took pride in making sure that he had all the work done, so that Jacob didn't have to. By the time he was finished his chores, he was famished, so he went in and made supper.

Jacob was still in bed when he got back into the house. He must have been really tired, because his afternoon naps didn't normally last so long. Billy decided to wait until supper was ready before he woke him.

"Something smells good out there. Pretty hard to sleep, with all those wonderful smells in the house," Jacob said from the other room.

"Let's hope it tastes as good as it smells then," Billy said.

"I'm sure it will. I always enjoy your cooking. I must have been tired, I can't believe I slept so long," Jacob said, shaking the sleep from his head.

He went to the sink and splashed some cold water on his face, towelled off and then sat at the table, waiting for supper to be served.

They had their supper together and then spent a relaxing evening out on the stoop, enjoying the beautiful weather and each other's company.

"Don't forget, I need you to drive me into town for my lawyer's appointment for nine o'clock tomorrow."

"Sure thing, I'll set my alarm," Billy said, laughing.

Jacob laughed at that too. They both knew that Billy was always up at the crack of dawn. He would have all his chores done, breakfast on the table and waiting for Jacob to roll out of bed. That's just the way Billy was, he never slept in.

True to form, the next morning Billy was up before the rooster crowed. He went straight to the barn and started on his chores. He finished them quickly, washed up and then made bacon and eggs, toast and coffee and then went to wake up Jacob.

He called to Jacob from the door, but he didn't respond.

"Come on sleepy head. I've done all the chores and made breakfast and you're still sleeping?" he said, laughing.

Jacob kept on sleeping. It was no surprise really. He had been sleeping later and later as the months passed and had been taking longer afternoon naps as of late.

"Come on. I know you don't like to be rushed, so you better get moving or you're going to be late for your appointment," Billy said, teasing Jacob.

Jacob still didn't stir, so Billy went and shook him gently. If Billy's Father was there, he would have identified with what Billy was now feeling. He had gone through it himself years ago, with his own Father and now it was Billy's turn.

Billy knew right away that his world had changed again for the worse, one more time. He knew before he ever laid eyes on him or took his pulse, that he was gone. Jacob moved unnaturally when he shook him and that told him everything he needed to know. He sat on the bed with his hand resting on Jacob's shoulder.

"Now you can rest Dad," he said quietly. "Now you can rest."

Billy sat in silence for a while, letting the surrealness of the moment catch up in his mind. He felt numb, unable to think or feel, to process what had happened. He laid down on the bed next to Jacob with his hand still on his shoulder. He thought about the day he met Jacob and the many conversations that they had had over the years. He couldn't remember them all of course, there were far too many, but he knew that he enjoyed each one of them. He thought about Frank and Abby and how poorly they treated their Father, and how he was going to have to call one of them now. He dreaded having to make that call, and so he put it off for as long as he could. He felt much the same way as he had when Henry died. He just wanted to spend some alone time with Jacob. This was certainly different. Billy would have to be completely naïve to believe that Jacob was going to live forever. He knew this day was coming and he tried to believe that it was years down the road. He didn't want to believe Jacob when he told him it was close at hand, but deep down, he knew. He was tired more often lately, even though he was sleeping more and he had been doing less and less chores around the farm. Jacob saw this day coming, and if Billy was honest with himself, he did as well. He didn't want to think about it then, and he didn't want to think about it now.

He just wanted to say his goodbyes, on his own terms and in his own time. Billy spent time talking to Jacob and then thinking some more. It gave him some peace, that maybe, just maybe Jacob was now with his beloved Margaret. He smiled at the thought. Jacob would be so happy, to be with her again.

Billy also thought about how wonderful a man that Jacob was and how blessed he felt, to have been a part of his life, for as long as he had been.

Finally, Billy had said his goodbyes and made peace with the situation. He took a few deep breaths and he found Frank's number and called him.

True to form, Frank seemed more bothered at the inconvenience of his Father's death, than he was sad to hear about it. Abby called him shortly after he got off the phone with Frank, and she acted in much the same manner.

"We'll be there first thing in the morning. Don't touch anything. We'll look after everything when we get there," Abby ordered.

"Whatever," Billy said and hung up the phone.

Billy was disgusted and he went to tell Jacob about it. When he had filled Jacob in about the conversations that he had had with his children, he called 911.

Ten minutes later two police cruisers and an ambulance showed up at the door. Everyone in town knew Billy by this point and they all knew the special bond that he and Jacob shared. They offered him their condolences and then went about their respective jobs. Billy had one last chance to say goodbye to his Dad, then they all left and took Jacob away with them.

Billy was left all alone in the big empty farmhouse. He went outside and worked hard for the remainder of the day, trying to finish anything and everything that needed to be done. Really, he was just trying to keep busy so he wouldn't think, so he wouldn't break down. An idle mind is the devil's playground, is what his Dad used to say.

This was different than when Henry had died. Billy wasn't the one responsible for one thing and Jacob was an old man, unlike Henry who had the rest of his life to look forward to. It sucked, no doubt about it, but it was easier to come to terms with. The hollow feeling that had begun creeping in immediately, wasn't present this time. Billy had grown and matured a lot since then. He was a different person now than he was. Henry would have been proud of how caring and thoughtful he had become, more like Henry was.

He finished his chores, far too quickly for his liking. He dreaded the thoughts of spending the night alone in the big farm house, without Jacob there to keep him company.

When he finally did go in, he turned on nearly every light in the house. It didn't seem so bad when Jacob was here but now that he was alone, it felt as though the darkness had weight to it, like it was pressing down on him. Nights were very dark, out in the country, away from the lights of town. It made Billy shiver just thinking about it.

He had a long, hot shower. He stood with his face turned upward for a very long time and even through the water flowing over his face, he could taste the salt from his tears.

He towelled off and sat naked on the toilet for a very long time. Memories of Jacob flooded through his tired mind, in no particular order. He stayed that way until his legs were numb. When he stood up he had to wait for a couple of minutes, until the blood rushed back in and the pins and needles in his legs dissipated. He got dressed, went to the refrigerator and stood looking past the food in front of him. He decided that he didn't have the patience, nor the appetite, or the desire to eat alone. He decided to go into town and grab a bite to eat there.

Even the drive into town seemed foreign to him, without Jacob sitting beside him, telling him one of his stories. He never minded listening to Jacob, and he never told him that he'd heard them all, many times before. He saw how much he enjoyed telling his tales and it made Billy feel good, just to see how happy it made him. What he wouldn't give to hear one of his stories now.

Billy drove slowly into town. He was in absolutely no hurry to get back to the empty farm house. Even as he drove, he started to think that it was a bad idea, after all. He didn't want to be alone out on the farm, but he didn't want to be around people either. He was in no mood to talk to anyone, to answer how he was doing, or if he needed anything. He pulled off to the side of the road, shut the truck off and got out to get some fresh air and clear his head.

After some time filling his lungs with the cool night air and staring up at the stars, his troubles seemed a little smaller and more manageable. He took one last, deep breath and climbed back into his truck. He paused for a moment, to remember the day that Jacob had given it to him. He was on top of the world and he never forgot, how grateful he was to have it. He realized that he was stroking the steering wheel, as if his truck were a living, breathing thing. He couldn't help it, he loved his truck. He smiled sadly, started the truck and continued the rest of the way into town.

He went into Angel's diner and ordered a burger, fries and a cola. He felt like everyone in the diner was staring at him.

"Look, there's that poor Billy Johnson," their eyes were saying.

Fortunately, it was a small crowd this evening and he didn't have to talk to anyone, except Lisa his server.

Lisa was a cute little thing, and normally he would be nervous around her.

He had thought about asking her on a date, but he never had the nerve. Tonight, was a different story. He barely saw her and he never cared at all, when she rubbed his shoulder while he ordered. She smiled kindly at him, took his order and left. She didn't pry and ask him stupid questions and he didn't notice at all. He was too busy carrying on, too busy just getting through the day.

He ate with his head down, not looking around, huddled over his meal like it was the most important thing in the world. When he was finished, he left some money on the table, got up and left. Lisa said something to him as he was leaving, but he was lost in thought and didn't hear her.

He drove home, laid on the couch and watched the television with the volume up to drown out his thoughts and to give some life to the big, old farm house.

CHAPTER TWELVE

The next morning he awoke on the couch, a little disoriented. It took him a moment to survey his surroundings and realize where he was. Someone was repeatedly, knocking loudly at the front door. It was unusual for him to sleep in and just as unusual for someone to be knocking at the door. Billy had a bad feeling, that he knew who it was.

"Are you going to let me in or am I going to stand out here all day?" she asked.

To be honest given the two options, Billy would have much preferred the second one.

"I'm coming!" he yelled.

He opened the front door to let her in. Jacob had always insisted that they lock the door when they were away, or home and sleeping. It was just one of the quirks that made Jacob who he was.

"It's about time!" Abby scowled, when he opened the door.

"I'm sorry, I've had a very bad night, as you can imagine," Billy said.

"Well, now that Dad is gone, your services will no longer be required. I'll give you some time to get your personal items and then I can call you a cab if you'd like," she said flatly.

"This is my home now. It has been for several years," Billy said.

"Not any longer. Just tell me what you are owed for your services and I'll settle up with you," Abby said.

"Jacob wasn't paying me! He was like a Dad to me and I was like a son to him."

"Humph," she scoffed. "My Dad had a son, Frank and a daughter, me. I know your kind, preying on the loneliness of an old man!" she said.

"It wasn't like that! Besides he wouldn't have been lonely, if you and your brother gave a shit about him!" Billy yelled.

Billy could feel the anger rising in him, something that hadn't happened in a couple of years. The closest he came was the day that he and Abby first met.

"Our relationship was complex and I don't need to defend my brother's or my relationship with our Father to you! Get your stuff and get out!" she yelled.

"I'm not going anywhere. This is my home and Dad said that neither you nor your brother gave a shit about this place, so he was going to leave it to me," Billy yelled.

"Oh, so that's what you were up to! It makes sense now! We'll see about that. I have the will with me and he left everything to Frank and me, his real kids!" she yelled.

"Call his lawyer if you don't believe me!" Billy screamed.

"No need, I've already talked to him. Dad has had the same will, for twenty years," she said snottily.

"I'm going to go see him myself, if you don't mind?" Billy said.

"I guess. it's up to you, but you'd better not think about skipping town. That truck belongs to the estate now."

"It's my truck, he gave it to me last year!" Billy yelled.

"According to my records, it's still in my Father's name."

Billy was furious. He wanted to strangle her on the spot, but instead, ran past her out the door and fled in his truck. He had to go see Jacob's lawyer, to see what he could do. He was beside himself with rage.

She had no idea what Jacob and Billy's relationship was like and she didn't care. She had no relationship with her Father, wouldn't give him the time of day, and now she was going to point her finger at him, saying that he was only after his money. He never met anyone that could infuriate him as much as she did.

Billy slammed his fist down hard on the steering wheel with disgust. Hopefully Jacob's lawyer could straighten all this out. He would love nothing more than to throw Abby out on her ass.

He was in a hurry to say the least, and never even noticed the police car that passed him, as he sped down the gravel road a couple of miles from the farm. The policeman spun the car around, turned on his lights and siren and chased after Billy. He was so focused on getting to the lawyer that he didn't even notice the police car following him. Finally, he heard the siren and he looked into his rear-view mirror. He slowed down immediately and began to pull on to the shoulder of the road.

Billy's heart was pounding, but it wasn't that he had just been pulled over. It was because he was in such an agitated state from the conversation with Abby.

"Why you in such a hurry, Billy?" Officer Hamilton asked.

"I'm sorry Dale. I just had the worst fight with Jacob's daughter Abby and I'm on my way to see his lawyer," Billy said.

"Well, that explains it then. She's a real piece of work that one. Listen, normally I'd ask for your license, registration and proof of insurance, but I know that you don't have a license and I know that Jacob would make sure that the insurance was up to date. What I need you to do, is slow down, Billy," Dale said.

"I will."

"You're lucky that it was me that stopped you. Some of the guys down at the station aren't quite as understanding as I am, so just be careful, alright? I'm gonna let you off with a warning. I know you're going through some shit right now; I can appreciate that."

"Thanks Dale."

"Everyone liked Jacob, he was a good man and I know he thought of you as his son. Hell, I think he liked you more than his own kids. I know he did. Anyway, slow down. Don't need you getting yourself killed. We already have Jacob to bury, don't need anyone else to add to that list. Take care Billy," he said.

"I will."

"I'll see ya at the funeral."

"Okay, I'll see ya, and thanks again."

"Don't mention it."

Dale turned and went back to his cruiser. He spun the car back around and headed in the direction he was going. Billy pulled back onto the road and continued on his way into town.

He arrived five minutes later and wasted no time getting out of his truck and running up the steps to the lawyer's office.

The receptionist took one look at him and held up her pointer finger, signalling for him to wait a minute. She scurried into the back and returned a few seconds later.

"He's expecting you, go right in Billy," she said.

"Hi Billy, come on in. Really sorry to hear about Jacob's passing. He was a good soul, as you well know. Listen, I'll cut right to it. Abby called me earlier today, so I know what brings you by. A real bitch that one! I wish there was something I could do, but my hands are tied. Real shitty timing for Jacob to have to go and die like he did. If he'd have waited until after you guys came to see me, well… we would be having a completely different conversation than we are right now," he said, shaking his head.

"I'm not too smart when it comes to legal mumbo jumbo, so if you don't mind, just tell me where I stand."

"Okay it's like this. Even though Jacob told me what his intentions were, he hadn't changed his will, as of the time of his death. The will I have on file leaves everything to Frank and Abby. I'm sorry Billy. I know it's not right, but there's nothing I can do about it."

"I understand. It's just that Dad didn't want them to have the farm, because he knew it meant nothing to them and they'll just sell it."

"The only thing I could do, is to try and get it so you can continue to live there, until it sells."

"That's okay. I don't want to be there with Abby breathing down my neck all the time. I think after the funeral, I'll just jump in my truck and drive, and wherever I end up, is where I end up," Billy said quietly.

The lawyer was looking at his feet now and shaking his head slowly from side to side.

"What's that for? What else?" Billy asked.

"Billy, I'm very sorry to have to tell you this, but even though Jacob gave you that truck, he never changed the ownership into your name. That means that it belongs to the estate. I'm sorry Billy," he said.

"So that's it, I'm fucked!" Billy yelled.

"I'm sorry Billy. Jacob couldn't have died at a more inopportune time. Believe me, I don't want those two getting the estate, but there is absolutely nothing I can do about it," he said.

"I understand. There's nothing you can do. I get it," Billy said quietly, as he walked dejectedly toward the door, head down, shoulders slumped forward.

"There are a lot of folks in town that have really come to like you Billy. I'm sure we can figure out a way to help you out. I'll talk to some people and see what we can come up with. It's the least I can do for you... and Jacob too," he said thoughtfully.

Billy didn't respond. He just continued walking, out of the office and down the street. He just kept going. He had no destination in mind, he just knew that his mind was weary, numb, and he needed to keep moving or go insane.

He thought terrible thoughts, of hurting Abby, hurting her badly. He kept walking, but he couldn't stop the thoughts. He put his hand over his ears and screamed loudly.

"Leave me alone! I just want to be left alone!" he yelled, at the top of his lungs, bent over at the waist. He had walked far enough that he was no longer in town and so no one was around to witness his outburst.

It wasn't just the thoughts in his head that he was trying to keep at bay. He could feel it pressing in on him like an enormous weight. It got heavier and heavier, until he thought that he would be crushed by it. He shook his head and yelled once again.

"Leave me alone! Just leave me alone!"

But it wouldn't leave him alone. It wouldn't be denied. It lay in waiting all this time, until he was at his most vulnerable, for the opportunity to consume him once again.

The hollowness spread over him like a dark cloud blotting out the sun. It filled him and left little room for anything happy or good. He could feel its despair, its hunger, its thirst for malevolence and pain. He could see the darkness and the heaviness of it and he knew what it wanted.

He fought it with everything that he had. He had come so far. He had built a new life for himself, a happy life. But it didn't care for such things. It knew only misery and despair and it knew that Billy was ripe for the taking.

Billy fell to his knees, overcome by the weight of it.

"I'm sorry Jacob! I tried, but I can't fight it! I'm not strong enough!" he called out, and fell over on his side unconscious.

Billy awoke to a dog licking his face. He held up his elbow to shield himself, but the dog re-positioned itself and continued to lick. Billy reached up quickly and grabbed the dog by the fur at the side of his head. He paused for a moment. The thought of letting him go, flickered behind his dull eyes. He sunk his thumbs into the dog's eye sockets. The dog yelped in pain and then began to bay and yelp more, as Billy sunk his thumbs deeper and deeper. Blood was now running down both of his hands and up his wrists. The dog fell silent and Billy raised it above him as though it were a trophy he had just won. A large grin spread across his face and he took several deep breaths, before discarding the dog unceremoniously to the ditch, beside the roadway.

He got to his feet. His heart was hammering wildly. Adrenaline coursed through his veins and he felt light-headed. He took some time to savour the moment. He raised his hands far above his head and welcomed the rush of warmth and soothing comfort that flooded into him, filling him up as it did. He turned and walked back toward town, to go get his truck, smiling and whistling as he did.

CHAPTER THIRTEEN

He jumped into his truck and drove back out to the old farmhouse. Abby met him at the door, ready for an argument, but he just smiled, brushed past her and went to his room. Abby looked as if he had slapped her across the face. Her reaction buoyed his spirits even more than they were already. He felt no remorse for what he had done to the poor dog at the side of the road. When the hollowness had a grip on him, nothing else mattered, it just wanted to be fed and what Billy wanted came a distant second.

Normally he would be on top of the world afterwards, but this time was different. He had just lost his Dad and that fact hadn't changed but all the other business about the farm, Abby, Frank and his truck, seemed to matter less than it had earlier. In his room, with the door shut on the outside world, he could almost believe that everything was okay and that it would all work out in the end. All he knew was that he had a funeral to prepare for and he had some things that needed to be said.

Billy sat down at his desk and began to write. He was never very good at writing, but that night the words jumped from his pen to the paper so quickly that he could barely keep up. His hand was starting to cramp but he dared not stop, for fear of the moment passing, and he would be left without the words to pay tribute to his Dad. He deserved that much. It's all he had to give, the only way he knew to honour him. When he had finished, there was a messy stack of papers scattered across his desk. He arranged them in some semblance of a pile and then placed a book on top of them to keep them from being disturbed.

He opened the window to let in the cool night breeze. He breathed deeply and remembered nights sitting out on the stoop, talking to Jacob about anything and everything. He missed him so much already. When it's your time to go, it's your time to go and that's it. Death waits for no man it seemed, he thought. Billy was reminded once again, just how unfair this world could be. How could a God govern over such a place? If he did, he would have to be an unjust God.

He took another deep breath. He knew there was no way he was going to be able to sleep any time soon, so he decided to pick out some clothes for Jacob to wear. He went quietly into his room, being careful not to alert Abby to his presence. He didn't want to have to deal with her right now. It wasn't so much that he dreaded the confrontation. It was because, he wasn't entirely sure that he could refrain from killing her.

He laid out his nice pin striped suit. He stuffed a yellow handkerchief in the left front pocket and set a black pair of shoes at the foot of the bed. Satisfied with his selection, he snuck back to his bedroom.

Once safely back in his room, he lay on his bed and stared at the ceiling. He was exhausted, after a long, trying day.

He must have dozed off, because a knock at his door, awakened him.

"Yes," he said curtly.

He knew who it was and he was in a bad mood before he even spoke.

"I see that there are clothes laid out on my Father's bed. I don't recall him ever wearing them before. Did you buy them recently?" she asked, through the door.

"No. He bought them several weeks ago in town."

"Oh, okay. Do you remember which store he bought them in?" she asked politely.

She was being far too friendly and Billy figured she must be up to something.

"Why?" Billy snarled.

"I'd like to take them back and buy something a little more appropriate for the occasion," she said.

Billy couldn't believe what he was hearing, the nerve of this woman. He didn't think it possible, but he hated her now, more than ever.

"Dad picked those clothes out himself, so like it or not, it was his choice and you're not going to change it," Billy said.

"We'll just see about that. Oh, and Billy, I want the keys to my Dad's truck. I don't want you running off with it, when I'm not looking," she said.

Billy was furious, instantly. No one could anger him, so quickly and completely as she could. He swung open the door and brushed past her, keys in hand. He had to get the Hell out of there, before he did something that he would regret. The local police might forgive him for a lot of indiscretions, but murder wasn't one of them.

He hurried toward the front door and she followed close on his heels, nattering at him as they went.

"Give me those keys. You're not going anywhere with that truck. I want them now. Do you hear me?"

Billy ignored her and made his way to his truck, jumped in and started it.

Abby stood in front of the truck. Billy swung his head around and threw it into reverse, but there was a wagon blocking his way from backing up.

"You're going to have to run me over, if you want to leave. Now give me those keys or I'm going to call the police!" she yelled.

Billy put the truck back into neutral and revved the engine.

"Ooh, big tough guy. What are you going to do now?" she taunted him.

Billy revved the engine again and Abby stood her ground, laughing smugly. Billy threw the truck into drive and brought his foot down hard on the gas pedal.

Abby's smug look changed to one of panic and then she was gone under the truck. The truck bounced high in the air as the back tires ran over her midsection. Billy looked in his rear-view mirror and saw Abby writhing in pain behind him. He spun the truck around to face her. She managed to lift her head from the ground and started screaming at him again. Billy rammed the gas pedal to the floor and aimed the driver's side wheel, right at her head. The truck careened wildly to the left when it made contact with her skull. There was a sickening, dull thud, followed by silence, glorious silence.

Billy turned the truck around to where Abby lay motionless in the middle of the yard. A long swath of bright red blood, lay ten feet out in front of her. Billy got out of the truck and walked over to where she lay. Her eyes were open and she was twitching slightly. Blood trickled from the corner of her mouth and her head was misshapen. He looked down on her with a satisfied look on his face, and smiled. He enjoyed the moment for as long as he could. A warm, content feeling washed over him and he realized that he had the largest erection that he had ever had. He reached down inside of his pants and grabbed his penis. His watch caught a few strands of pubic hair as he did.

The pain caused him to wake instantly. He was still holding his penis, and he still had the largest erection of his life. He went into the bathroom so that he could masturbate. He thought of how Abby looked lying in the yard and how she had finally fallen silent and he finished quickly in one of the most satisfying climaxes, that he had ever experienced.

He just finished cleaning himself off, when a knock came to the bathroom door.

"Are you going to be in there for ever? I have to pee really badly," Abby said.

"Be out in a minute," Billy said, laughing to himself. He didn't think that Abby would find the humour in it.

He reached his hand out to grab hold of the vanity. He was a little light headed and his legs felt a little rubbery. He stood like that for a moment, trying to compose himself, before opening the door.

"Come on! What's taking you so long? Hurry up!" she demanded.

Billy thought for a moment of letting her wait and letting her piss herself, right there in the hallway. He decided that listening to her bitch wasn't worth it, so he opened the door.

She was standing with one hand on her hip and the other was in the midst of knocking again. The door opening, startled her a bit and she jumped. Billy smirked, as he pushed past her.

"What's so funny?" she asked.

She was someone who was used to getting her own way and it bothered her badly when she thought that someone might be hiding something from her. Apparently, she forgot about having to pee for the moment and followed Billy down the hall, like a little puppy.

Billy never answered her. He just continued walking down the hall and when he reached his bedroom, he closed the door in her face.

"Nice, real nice. Well we won't have to put up with each other much longer. After the funeral is over, your business here is finished and you can leave. Do you hear me?" she yelled, through the closed door.

Billy responded by turning on his stereo to drown her out. He had no real interest in listening to music but he didn't want to hear her screeching voice any longer either. He decided to sneak out and go back into town for an early breakfast.

He opened his door slowly and crept down the hall. He could hear her muttering to herself through the closed bathroom door. She never stopped talking. Billy thought that she probably talked in her sleep. He couldn't believe that her husband could stand living with her. She had only been at the farm for a day and he felt like killing her already. He thought back to his dream and to her lying in the dirt with her eyes wide and her mouth open, but silent, and he grinned widely. Some of that feeling washed through his body once again. He shuddered and smiled wider still.

He jumped into his truck and began his drive to town. He drove slowly, savouring every minute behind the wheel. He stroked the steering wheel tenderly. He even found himself talking to her. He was saying his goodbyes. He knew their time was short and he wanted to enjoy every last moment that he could.

All too quickly, he arrived in town and pulled up to Angel's diner. He turned the truck off and sat for a while listening to the radio. He put his head down on the steering wheel and just enjoyed being in his truck.

A loud knock on the window startled him. He jerked his head back quickly and sat up. He turned his head toward the window and rubbed at the back of his neck.

"I'm sorry. I didn't mean to startle you," Lisa said.

Billy rolled the window down. His face was red with embarrassment.

"Deep in thought, I guess. Didn't see you sneak up on me," he said quietly.

"I'm not surprised, with all that's been going on lately. I'm very sorry to hear about Jacob's passing; he was such a kind man. Everyone loved him dearly, he'll be sorely missed," she said, tears coming to the corners of her eyes.

"That's very kind of you to say. He was like a Father to me," Billy said thoughtfully.

"Well, I have to get to work. Are you coming in for breakfast?" she asked, smiling warmly.

"Yeah, I need to be away from the farm for a while. Jacob's daughter Abby is there and she is driving me insane."

"Great! I'll see you inside." Lisa said, as she reached out to rub his shoulder.

She spun quickly and headed toward the front door of the diner. Her short skirt flung in the air when she turned, revealing her bright white panties. She took a peak over her shoulder to see if Billy was looking.

Billy blushed, and Lisa gave a cute little laugh at the sight of it. He tried to look as if he hadn't noticed, but failed miserably. His face was fire engine red and beads of sweat stood on his brow. He felt an excitement that he had never experienced before. He had a large erection once again, only this time it was different.

When he entered the diner, Lisa came over quickly and escorted him to a booth. She was still smiling, and now it was her turn to blush a little.

He had seen Lisa in here many times before, but had only noticed her in passing. Lisa on the other hand had been trying to get his attention for some time now, but he never seemed interested, until today.

How couldn't he have noticed her before? She had a great personality and a wonderful smile. She was petite but also a little athletic looking. She might have been a cheerleader or a gymnast, when she was in high school. She had long blonde hair that was pulled back at the moment and she had the darkest blue eyes that Billy had ever seen.

Billy, for his part was no slouch either. Years of hard work on the farm had made him quite muscular. The kind of long, lean muscle that you get from work and not from body- building. His hair was longer now, than it had ever been before, but it was well groomed and always clean. Billy hated when his hair got greasy and sometimes he washed his hair twice a day, when the weather was warm. His hair was chestnut brown but the sun had lightened it some and he now had streaks throughout that were nearly blonde. He was always clean shaven. He hated the way whiskers felt on his face, especially when he was sweating while he worked. He had a strong jawline that he shared with his Father and Grandfather, but he was taller than them and his facial features were more chiseled than theirs. They had rounder faces and larger noses than he did. His face was slimmer and his nose was smaller like his Mom's. Put it all together and Billy had grown into quite a handsome young man.

For whatever Billy Johnson was, he was never conceited. He was a bit of an introvert and he was humble, giving and kind, now.

That was of course when he wasn't overtaken by the hollowness. When that happened, all bets were off. When it came calling, there was no telling what Billy was capable of.

It had been pushed deep down inside him for now, but it was never truly gone. It would lie in waiting for years if need be, but it would be willing to take charge whenever or wherever an opportunity presented itself. It was patient. It would have its time again.

CHAPTER FOURTEEN

Billy smiled at the thought of Lisa, but his dry, cracked lips, screamed in pain as he did. It brought his thoughts crashing back to the reality of his present situation. Oh, what he wouldn't give to hold Lisa in his arms one last time. To see her warm smile and to smell her sweet perfume. To see her play with the hair tucked behind her ears whenever she got nervous or to hear her laugh. What he wouldn't do to see her. If only he could do it all over. Not just things with Lisa but with his life.

The sun had begun its descent into the darkness. It would be hours yet, but it was coming all the same. He was okay with it. He had made peace with it and was no longer afraid. In fact, there was nothing that could scare him now. People got scared when they were afraid of being hurt, or killed, or of the unknown. Billy had nothing left to lose and he was beginning to believe that the world would be a better place without him in it. Suffering followed him everywhere he went and he was tired. He was tired of hurting those that he loved, of hurting people when the hollowness overtook him, but mostly, he was just tired.

He thought back again to that day at the diner. He could picture Lisa's beautiful face. He remembered everything about that day. How could he possibly forget? She was the love of his life and he missed her so.

CHAPTER FIFTEEN

Lisa served him his breakfast and then stayed to talk to him for a bit as he ate.

"Someday, when I can afford it, I'm leaving here and going somewhere new. It doesn't matter where; I just need a change of scenery. I can get a job in any crappy diner, anywhere. I've saved enough money to buy a car and as soon as I save a little more for spending money, I'm going to leave and never come back."

Billy listened intently to everything that she had to say. Her voice was soft and as beautiful as she was. He could have listened to her talk all day.

"Lisa! Are you going to look after the other customers today?" her boss yelled, from behind the counter.

"Oh shit, I'd better go. I'm working a short shift today. I'm filling in for Denise, but only until lunch. Do you want to do something when I'm done?" she asked.

"Lisa! Orders up!" her boss yelled, sounding more impatient now.

"Sounds good. I'll come back later. You'd better go before you get yourself in trouble," Billy said.

"Okay see ya later," she said, spinning quickly and heading toward the counter.

She took a peek over her shoulder once again, and of course Billy was looking. She bounced over to the counter and picked up the order.

•   •   •   •   •

When he was finished his breakfast, he left some money on the table, including a nice tip for Lisa and went outside.

He had a large wad of cash in his pocket that he was afraid to leave back at the farm, for fear of Abby finding it and claiming it as hers, like everything else. Jacob hadn't really paid him for the work he had done over the years, per se, but he did give him an allowance of sorts. Once in a while, he would give him a few hundred dollars for spending money, and over the course of the past two plus years it had added up to a reasonable amount of money. He tucked the money deep into his pocket and decided to go for a walk, until Lisa was done work.

Everywhere he went in town, there was someone that waved to him or stopped to talk for a while, and quite often the conversation turned out to be about Jacob. It seemed everyone knew how great a man Jacob was except for his own kids. It was nice to hear everyone talk about Jacob and tell their own stories about him. It felt for a short time anyway, that he was with Billy once again. He missed him so much already and he wasn't sure how he was going to make it through the funeral service tomorrow, but he knew that he had to remain strong, until he delivered his speech. After that, he could fall apart, but not until then. It was very important that he honoured him properly and did him proud. Billy's real Father would understand. He was unable to deliver the speech at his Dad's funeral. His sister had to do it for him and he never forgave himself for that.

The time passed by quickly and before he knew it, he had run out of time and was late getting back to the diner, but only by a couple of minutes.

Lisa was waiting in front when he arrived, and she waved enthusiastically from the other side of the road. He crossed the road to where she was standing.

"Glad to see you came back."

"I never actually left. I've been visiting with everyone in town. It seems they all want to talk about Jacob; everyone has a story to tell."

"No question, we all loved Jacob. What wasn't there to love?" Lisa said.

"So, what do you want to do?" Billy asked.

"Well, I'm parked just around the corner. Do you want to take my car, or your truck?"

"My truck, if you don't mind. Abby is going to make me give it back soon and sell it with the estate, so I want to drive it as much as I can before that happens."

"Fine by me. Let's go," she said, making her way to the other side of the truck.

"Okay where are we going?"

"You'll see. Just follow this road straight west, until you run out of road."

"But that is over an hour drive from here."

"You have somewhere else you need to be?" she asked, smiling.

"No," Billy said. He couldn't think of any place in the entire world that he would rather be, than with her.

Lisa was like a breath of fresh air. She was full of life and energy. She smiled and laughed while she talked and her upbeat personality was exactly what Billy needed. He was a lot more reserved than she was. He bordered on brooding, at times. Billy hadn't had a lot of moments to celebrate in his life, and happy times were few and far between.

Lisa loved to talk and as it turned out, Billy was an excellent listener. It fit his calm and somewhat reflective demeanor. Plus, he just loved the energy and passion in her voice when she spoke.

Lisa was raised by her Grandma after her Mom passed from cancer, when she was only seven. Her Grandmother was very loving and she was always there when Lisa needed a shoulder to cry on, or when she wanted to share a happy moment with her. She was her tower of strength and emotional support. She could always count on her to say just the right thing. It wasn't always what she wanted to hear, but it was what needed to be said, at the time. Sadly, she passed away two years ago, and Lisa missed her a great deal.

Billy thought, Lisa probably told him that story because of what had happened with Jacob. He felt an immediate connection with her because of it. She kept her story light and positive somehow and Billy could feel the love and admiration that she had for her Grandma. He thought, that if he had to tell the same story, it would be dark and gloomy. He liked her version much better.

"I've been doing all of the talking. I'm sorry, sometimes I don't know when to shut up. Tell me about yourself Billy Johnson. What brought you to our small town in the first place? I remember the first time that you came into the diner with Jacob, like it was yesterday. Your hair wasn't as long then and you weren't as strong as you are now," she said, squeezing his shoulder, as if to prove her point.

"I don't mind telling you that I had a crush on you. I've been waiting for this moment for a long time. Oh God, that sounded a little creepy. I'm not a stalker or anything. I just mean that you certainly made an impression on me, right from the start," she said, hiding her face in her hands, and shaking her head.

"Okay, I'm going to shut up now before I completely embarrass myself," she said, peaking from between her fingers.

"I don't know what to say. I know that I'm not as comfortable talking about myself as you are. It takes me a while before I feel comfortable enough, you know?" Billy said.

·　　·　　·　　·　　·

"Tell me about your parents, start there. Or what your favourite food is. I know you like burgers, but are they your favourite? Or do you have any brothers or sisters. What makes you happy? What do you like to do in your spare time? That kind of thing. What makes Billy Johnson tick?" she said, falling silent, waiting intently for his answers to the riddle, of who is Billy Johnson.

"I'll start with my favourite food, which is lasagna. I don't want to start with my family because that is just too depressing and I don't think I could tell that story, without it becoming something negative. So, I'll save that for another time, if you don't mind? My favourite colour is dark purple, and I'm not really sure what my favourite thing to do in my spare time is. Until recently that was easy. Jacob and I would sit out on the back stoop of the farmhouse for hours talking. That was my favourite thing in the whole world to do. I loved his stories, his wit and the passion in his voice when he spoke, much like when you were telling your story earlier."

"You really loved him, didn't you?" she asked, reaching up to rub Billy's shoulder, to comfort him.

Billy reached up unconsciously and grabbed her hand in his, and held it. When he realized what he had done, he went to let it go but she squeezed his hand and then continued to hold it as she lowered it to her lap.

"I loved him, and I miss him so much already, that I don't know what to do. I miss my brother Henry as well, but this is a newer, fresher wound that needs some time to heal," he said, beginning to tear up.

"Why don't you pull over for a minute?" she said quietly.

Billy was already in the process of doing just that. He pulled onto the shoulder of the road and shut off the truck.

"Come on. Let's get out for a minute and get some fresh air," she said, opening her door and jumping onto the gravel.

Billy got out and reluctantly went to the other side of the truck, while Lisa sat on the grass with her legs hanging over the edge of the ditch.

"Come, sit beside me," she said, patting the grass.

"I got a lot of advice from my Grandma, and one of the best things that she ever told me was this. Everyone grieves in their own way and in their own time, but we all have to grieve. You have to allow yourself to grieve Billy, and I think that you are ready to do so," she said.

She tucked her one leg up underneath her, so that she could turn and face him. She wrapped her arms around his neck and pulled herself close to him and rubbed her arms up and down his back.

She whispered in his ear. "You deserve to grieve Billy. It doesn't mean you're weak, it means you are human. Now let it out, just let it out," she said, while continuing to rub his back.

Billy's eyes welled with tears and he tried for a moment to hold them back but he found that he couldn't. He found that he didn't want to, and before long he was crying.

"There, there. Let it out," Lisa said soothingly, as she held him tightly.

Billy cried for several minutes. He felt safe in Lisa's arms. He didn't feel embarrassed but he did feel extremely relieved. It was like a huge weight had been removed, one that he didn't realize that he was carrying, until it was gone.

"Thank you," he simply said, when he was through.

"Don't mention it," she said, squeezing his hand and then jumping back into the truck.

"Now let's get going. We still have another twenty minutes of driving ahead of us."

Billy was relieved that she didn't make it into a bigger deal than it was. She understood that he needed to let it out, and that after he did, he could start to move forward.

The rest of the ride was completely different for Billy. He talked her ear off, instead of the other way around. He told her where he came from and about how his Mom died when he was young. He talked mostly about Henry though, and to his surprise his story was upbeat, positive, and fun. He laughed as he recounted many of the stories of Henry and himself getting into trouble together, when they were young.

"I'm glad that you feel comfortable enough to open up to me. I can really see the difference in you. It's like a weight has been lifted from your shoulders. I like you Billy and I'm really happy that we decided to do this," she said.

"Me too. The only other person that I've felt this comfortable with right away, was Jacob. And, you're right, I do feel much better. Thank you."

"Don't mention it."

They arrived at their destination in what seemed like seconds and Billy parked the truck on a small patch of dirt alongside the roadway.

"Come on! Follow me!" Lisa said, running down a path and into the woods.

By the time Billy rounded the corner and entered the path, she was gone, but he could hear giggling up ahead. He followed the winding path until it opened onto a small grassy area, where Lisa was standing looking back at him. Billy stopped where he was, to enjoy the view. The ocean lie before them. He could smell the salt air and hear the waves hitting the cliff far below. It wasn't the ocean that had him mesmerized though. Lisa was standing on the edge of the cliff, wearing nothing more than her bra and panties.

"I never thought to bring my bathing suit. I hope that this is okay," she said, raising her arms above her head and then pointing at her under garments.

"It's perfectly fine by me, but what if someone comes by?" Billy asked.

"Most people are working right now, besides we won't be here long, if you'd hurry up and join me," she said, laughing.

Billy went over to where she was and looked over the edge, to the ocean far below.

"Are you sure about this; you've done this before?" Billy asked.

"Lots of times. Now give me your clothes and I'll hide them in the bushes with mine, just in case someone does come along," she said, holding her hands out.

"I really have nothing to compare it to, but do you normally strip down to your undies on a first date?" Billy asked.

"God no! I hope you don't get the wrong idea about me. I've never done anything like this before."

"That makes two of us."

He took off his shirt quickly enough but he paused for a moment, before removing his pants.

"Come on! What's the difference between underwear and bathing suits really? Different material and different names, that's about it. Now give me your pants sir," she said, making a gimme gesture with both hands.

Billy took off his pants and reluctantly handed her his clothes, which she hid in the bushes alongside hers. She then ran back to where he stood, wearing only his underwear.

"That's a good look for you," she said.

"Right back at ya."

"Too late now, but you aren't afraid of heights, are you?" Lisa asked.

"No, not really," Billy said, peering over the cliff to the ocean, some fifty feet below. "You've done this before, right?"

"Used to come here all the time with my cousins. Don't worry, it'll be fine. Hey Billy, If I asked you to jump off a cliff, would you?" she said, smiling devilishly and grabbed his hand.

Billy didn't answer, but of course he would. He thought, at that moment he would do just about anything she asked him to do.

"Don't think about it, just do it okay. On the count of three. One! Two! Three!" she yelled, and pulled him with her, when she reached three.

They went hurtling down toward the water. Billy's free hand was flailing wildly through the air and his other hand gripped hers tightly. He was screaming the entire way down, but did just manage to get his mouth closed in time to avoid swallowing a mouthful of sea water. He went down and down under the water and he let go of Lisa's hand so he could swim to the surface. He came up gasping for air. He was short of breath, more from the excitement than from holding his breath under water. Lisa was already swimming for the rocks on shore. She looked back at him and laughed.

"I still remember my first time! You did pretty well, all things considered."

Billy didn't have the extra breath to answer her, he just swam to the rocks, where she had already pulled herself up and out of the water.

"Here, I'll give you a hand," she said, reaching out her hand, for him to grab.

"Just give me a second, my legs feel a little rubbery from all the adrenaline."

Lisa sat down on the rock and laughed. "So, what did you think?"

"It was awesome! We're going to do it again, right?"

"As many times as you want. Come on let's go," she said, reaching out her hand once again.

This time Billy accepted her hand, and she helped pull him up, onto the rock.

Billy followed her up the path to the top of the cliff. Her white panties and bra were nearly see-though because of the water. He was wearing blue underwear so that wasn't a problem but he was trying hard to think of other things, beside how beautiful Lisa looked. It would be very embarrassing to get to the top of the cliff and be sporting a huge woody. He made it to the top, and she never noticed a thing, or at least she never let on, anyway.

They jumped maybe ten more times that afternoon, before they'd both had enough. They sat on the edge of the cliff talking, while they dried, before retrieving their clothes from the bushes. They got dressed and then sat on the grass looking out over the ocean. The rhythmic sound of the waves hitting the rocks, and the sounds of the seagulls circling above, were hypnotic.

Lisa lay her head on Billy's shoulder and grabbed his hand in hers. He squeezed it slightly.

"Ouch!" she said,

"Sorry. Did I squeeze too hard?"

"Yeah, on our first jump, when you were holding on for dear life," she said, laughing.

"Sorry," Billy said, laughing as well.

"I know you would never hurt anyone intentionally," she said, leaning forward and kissing him. "We should get going, I'm starving. Aren't you?"

"I hadn't really thought about it, but yeah, I guess I am," he said, sounding a little distant. He shivered at the thought of what she had said. He followed her down the path, quietly thinking.

"Are you okay?" she asked.

"Just a little cold, that's all."

"Well I have the cure for that," she said, pressing her body tight to his and kissing him. "Come on, I thought we were leaving," she said giggling, as she jumped into the truck.

"Right behind you," Billy said.

They talked comfortably, for the entire ride back to town. Billy felt as at ease with her, as he had when he first met Jacob, and her body-language told him, that she felt the same way.

"Drop me off at my car if you don't mind. You can follow me to my house if you want and I'll fix us something to eat."

"Okay, sounds good," Billy said.

Billy followed her to her house, where as promised, she fixed them something to eat.

"I hope you're okay with a sandwich, I haven't gotten groceries yet," she said, and then proceeded to make a wonderful ham sandwich, with pickles, cheese and mustard on twelve-grain bread.

"I'm sorry, but I can't stay long. I want to go over the eulogy that I wrote, before the funeral tomorrow," Billy said, after they ate and talked for a while.

"I understand. Do you want some company tomorrow? I'm going to the funeral anyway. I think everyone is, as a matter of fact. I could go with you, it might help," she said awkwardly.

"I would like that. I'll come by and pick you up around 1 o'clock."

He waved to her as he drove out of her laneway and she stood waving back, until he was out of sight. I should have kissed her goodnight, I'm such an idiot, he thought.

CHAPTER SIXTEEN

Billy returned to the farm and Abby wasn't there. He was happy for her absence for sure, but he didn't think that even she could bring him down. He knew that he had to prepare for his Dad's funeral, but for now he was going to sit back and relax on the stoop and recall the events of the day.

He opened a nice cold beer and sat in Jacob's rocker. He took a few sips and then got up and moved to the chair, that he normally sat in. It felt unnatural to sit in Jacob's chair, like he was betraying him. He looked around, at the cracked, weathered boards of the stoop, that he meant to replace, but hadn't found the time. The little table that Jacob used to sit his tea on was pushed off to the side, never to be used again. He looked out over the farm yard. From here he could see the barn that he had painted the first year he was here. He could see the rolling fields laid out before him and he could just catch a glimpse of the corner of the pond off to his right. It was a very peaceful place to be. The crickets and peepers would sing to them every night as they sat there, talking about all manners of things, but it was Jacob's company that he cherished the most.

He settled in and continued to sip at his beer. He smiled unconsciously, lost in thought. It was one of the best days of his life, if not, the best day of his life.

He finished his drink and then sat for a while longer, enjoying the cool night air, but before long, he heard the sound of an approaching car in the distance. So much for enjoying the evening in peace, he thought, as he got up and went into his bedroom.

The car pulled up and he heard voices coming up the stoop and into the house. He identified the one as Abby's, hers was unmistakeable, the other he wasn't so sure about. It made sense that it was probably Frank's though. He hadn't seen Frank since he and Jacob had gone into the city to visit them.

Abby was an absolute bitch, no denying it. Frank on the other hand, didn't seem as bad. Abby only cared about herself and she didn't try to hide the fact. Frank was just busy with life and didn't visit his Father as much as he should have, but al least he wasn't outwardly hostile. When Abby was around however, he did let her push him around, so things tended to go in the direction that she wanted. He was sure that Frank must be sick of fighting her and succumbed to her nattering, just to shut her up.

Billy kind of understood, after all, his relationship with his brother was kind of like that. Henry rarely got to do what he wanted to, usually it was what Billy had planned.

He turned on the stereo in his room, to drown out the sound of Abby's voice. A few minutes later there was a knock at his door. He hesitated for a few seconds, thought about not answering the door, but like Frank he didn't want to get Abby going. He would play nice for now and hope she went away quickly.

Billy turned off the stereo, opened the door slowly and was surprised to find Frank standing there, instead of Abby.

"How's it goin' Billy?" Frank said.

"Oh, hi Frank. I was expecting it to be your sister," Billy said.

"Abby had to go back into town for something. I thought it would give us a chance to talk."

"To be honest, I'm glad she's gone." Billy said.

"Listen, I know what Abby can be like. She has convinced herself that you were just out to get Dad's money. For the record, I don't think that at all. Actually, I'm not so sure that she believes it entirely."

"Well, she could have fooled me."

"I think that she might be a little jealous of your relationship with our Father, that's all. I feel terrible that I didn't come to visit more often. I was just so busy with work and the kids. One week turned into months, and before I knew it six months or more had gone by. I know Dad was upset that we didn't come to visit more often."

"He missed you guys a lot."

"I know," he said, pausing, before continuing.

"I'm a little jealous myself, of the bond that you shared with Dad, but sadly I have no one to blame but myself. Abby said that Dad wanted to leave you the farm?" Frank said, just kind of stopping mid-thought.

"Yeah, he had made the lawyer appointment, but he died before he could go," Billy said sadly.

"I see. Well, there's not much I can do, unfortunately. Abby and I are both executors of the will and I can't do anything without her consent. I can try to talk to her, but I doubt it will do much good. Maybe you can stay on for a while, here at the farm," Frank said.

"That's okay, after the funeral, I think I'm just going to move on and see where I end up."

"Well, okay then. I'm going to get her to agree, to you keeping the truck, at least. I know Dad wanted you to have it, because he told me so himself, the last time I spoke to him on the phone," Frank said.

Billy's eyes lit up at that. "That would be great if you could do that! Thank you, Frank," Billy said.

"It's the least I could do. I wish I could do more. I'll let you get back to whatever you were doing."

"I was just about to go over my speech for tomorrow. You wouldn't want Abby to catch you talking to the enemy, anyway," Billy said, laughing dryly.

"Yeah, no kidding. Take care Billy."

"You bet! You too Frank, and thanks."

"Like I said, it's the least I could do," Frank said sullenly.

Billy believed Frank, that he would do more, if he could. He was sure that he would stop a long way short of giving him the farm, but he believed him all the same. He felt a little better about his situation now and he was glad that Frank had taken the time to talk to him.

Billy went to the desk and found the papers that he had written his speech on. He read it over in his head several times, making little changes here and there, until he was completely satisfied. He wasn't sure if he would be able to deliver it without breaking down but he knew that he had a better chance now, than he did before he had talked to Lisa. She had helped him deal with the sadness that he was feeling and at least now he had a fighting chance.

He put his speech away and got ready for bed. He lay there for some time, thinking about Jacob as he drifted off to sleep. Surprisingly, with everything that had happened lately, he slept a dreamless sleep.

In the morning, he awoke, ready to take on the day. Billy was dreading what lie ahead, but at the same time, he wanted to get on with it and get to the other side, to tomorrow.

Jacob wanted a simple funeral service with only close family and friends. He made a list of those people that were welcome at the funeral home. Everyone was welcome at the church service and internment, but he didn't want every Tom, Dick and Harry parading by to gawk at him in his casket. His list had to pass Abby's inspection, of course.

Billy went over his speech one last time. He wanted it to be perfect. It was the last thing that he could do for his Dad and he didn't want to let him down.

He puttered around his room for a bit, wasting time. He had breakfast and a shower and then paced back in forth in his room a little more. He could hear Abby and Frank talking in the kitchen, but he couldn't make out what they were saying. He heard Abby's voice getting louder and louder and then he heard the front door slam. He opened his door cautiously and stepped into the hall. All was quiet on the western front, so he continued down the hall and into the kitchen.

Frank was sitting at the kitchen table with his head in one hand and a glass of whiskey in the other.

"Oh, hey Billy. Want some?" he said, holding up his glass.

"No thanks, I'm good."

"Sometimes I swear I'd like to wring her neck. I know, I don't have to tell you what she can be like," Frank said quietly.

Nope he sure didn't. Every interaction with her that he had ever had, ended with him wanting to wring her neck, or worse. He thought about the dream that he had had and smiled a little.

"It's okay, she'll come around. I'll make sure you get that truck Billy. I promise," he said, and downed the glass of whiskey.

"Thanks Frank. Easy on that stuff, have a big day ahead of us. I'm going to go for a walk so I can clear my head," Billy said.

"You're probably right," he said, putting the cap back on the bottle and pushing it away from him.

He went outside and thankfully, Abby was nowhere to be seen. She must have gone into town, because her car wasn't in the yard.

Billy walked around the perimeter of the farm and visited the barn and all the out buildings. The weeds had grown tall along the fences and he made a mental note, that they needed to be cut back. He stood in the middle of the pasture, looking west. From there he could see the entire farm laid out before him. The gentle slope, the rolling hills and the forest that marked the end of Jacob's land. The large maple still stood in the middle of the pasture. Jacob had planted it the year that he bought the farm. It had served as shade for countless animals over the years. There were two cows and a goat presently enjoying the coolness that it provided.

He was saying his farewells. Jacob was a big part of why he loved this place but that wasn't the only reason. He had done a lot of hard work here and he enjoyed every minute of it. The farm was like a living, breathing being to him. Abby would look at it and see grass and trees and dirt, but Billy saw much more than that. There were the countless hours spent here with Jacob, and later, all the hours he spent here alone. When you spend that much time on the land, you can't help but get attached to it.

As he walked the farm, something occurred to Billy. He hated to think this way, but sometimes he couldn't help what things forced their way into his mind, when he wasn't careful. He wanted to hate Abby because she deserved it, but he wondered how she ended up the way that she did, and to a lesser extent how Frank ended up the way he did. He thought about it all the way back to the house and he could come up with only one conclusion. I guess you could say that he reached an epiphany of sorts. He made his way back to his room and got out the speech that he had spent so much time on. He set in on the desk and then got out two fresh pieces of paper and set them beside the other two. He paused for a moment, and then began to write.

CHAPTER
SEVENTEEN

After her argument with Frank, Abby went for a drive to clear her head. It took her past many familiar places that she remembered from her childhood. She drove past her old public school and later by the high school where she spent four long years. She was never a very popular kid during high school. She was awkward at that age, skinny, she wore glasses and had braces. All this combined to diminish her confidence and people tend to treat you like you treat yourself. She had few very close friends and during that time, it was her Mom who was the only one that she could really talk to.

She drove past the arena where she spent many days as a child taking figure skating lessons. She stopped for a minute to visit the swimming hole down the road from the farm where Frank and she spent many hot summer days as kids. The pond on the farm was spring fed and always too cold for her liking. All her memories were of things that she did with her Mom or Frank. Her Dad wasn't around much when they were kids. He was very busy with the farm during the growing season. He worked from sunrise to supper time and then went back out to feed the animals, clean their stalls and by the time he came back into the house, it was past her bedtime. She saw her Dad at breakfast and supper and on special occasions and very little time in between. In the winter, he got a job in town shovelling snow and so she didn't see him much then either. Her Mom did her best to explain to her and Frank that their Father had to work like that to pay for the farm, but that it wouldn't always be like that. As soon as he got ahead of the game then he would have more time for them. They just had to be patient, it wouldn't last for ever. Months went by and then years, but Jacob never seemed to get ahead of the game. Frank and Abby spent all their time with their Mom.

She remembered the day very well, that everything was supposed to change. Mom was very excited. She took Abby and Frank into town to buy new clothes to wear to the party they were throwing at the farm that evening. She pressed her Mom to find out what the big secret was and what the party was for, but her lips were sealed. Her Mom was floating on air. Abby had never seen her in such a giddy mood and it lasted the entire day.

They got back to the farm at about four o'clock and Dad met them at the door. He had traded his customary faded jean coveralls for a navy-blue suit. That wasn't what she noticed first, however. It was the huge smile on his face that she remembered so well. He ushered them into the living room, turned and announced.

"Things are going to be different around here from now on!"

Frank and Abby exchanged glances. They still had no idea what was going on.

"What's going on? Did we win the lottery or something?" Abby asked.

"No, no. You'll see. You'll just have to be patient," Jacob said.

"Why? What's the secret?" Frank asked.

"You'll see. It's a big deal; something to be proud of," Mom said.

"The caterers should be arriving any minute. You guys go get dressed and I'll start setting up," Jacob said.

They all went to their respective bedrooms to get changed, but Frank and Abby still didn't have a clue what was going on.

"What do you think is happening?" Abby whispered to Frank, as she stuck her head into his bedroom.

"Not sure, but I guess we'll know soon enough. Now go get ready," Frank said.

Abby wasn't normally one for being told what to do, but she knew that the sooner she got ready, the sooner she would find out what was going on.

They very rarely even went out for dinner. Everything that they ate was raised on the farm. Her parents considered it a waste of money to pay for food that they could make at home for a quarter of the price. Once in a while, they would go into town for ice cream in the summer, but those times were very few and far between.

Now they were getting supper catered in, not only for them, but for their extended family and some close friends as well. Whatever it was, it had to be big.

Abby changed quickly and ran a brush through her hair, just to say that she had, and then ran out to the living room. Frank showed up about the same time as she did, just in time to watch the caterers setting up, under Dad's watchful eye.

They wasted no time. They had perfected their craft after having set up for countless parties, weddings, funerals, baby showers etc. They were in and out in no time at all and the guests started arriving almost immediately.

"So, what's going on?" Abby asked, tugging at her Mom's elbow.

"Patience is a virtue my dear. You'll just have to wait. Now come with me to the front door to greet our guests. You too!" she said to Abby and then to Frank respectively.

Dad stood at the front of the line with Mom, then Frank and then Abby. They greeted everyone as they came filing past and into the house. There was a steady diet of "I haven't seen you in a month of Sundays," or "Wow, look how big you've gotten."

Abby was so happy when that part was over and she was allowed to be seated at the table.

Once everyone had taken their places and the murmuring subsided, Dad stood up, cleared his throat and waited for the last of the conversations to subside, before he began to speak.

"I want to thank all of our dearest relatives and friends for coming on this special night. It has long been custom in these parts to host such an event once the mortgage has been paid in full and I for one believe it to be a grand tradition. I'm so glad that all of you could find the time, to help us celebrate such a joyous occasion. So, without further ado. Let's eat. Oh, I'm sorry, not yet. Harold put your fork down!" he said, and everyone laughed.

"I want to thank my wonderful wife Margaret. Without her, none of this would have been possible. She is the kindest, most supportive wife and Mother that anyone could ever have hoped for and I'm sure I speak for the children as well, when I say we love you and thank you from the bottom of our hearts.

Margaret my dear, do you have anything that you would like to say?" Jacob asked.

She was wiping tears from her eyes and she just waved her hand, motioning him to continue.

"Okay, I guess, now we can eat. Hold on Harold, not so fast. We have to say grace first," Jacob said, and everyone laughed again.

Harold put down his fork, bowed his head along with everyone else, and Margaret said grace.

Supper was delicious and so was dessert. Everyone was laughing and talking and it was so nice to see her parents laughing and having such a good time as well. Abby couldn't recall ever seeing her parents enjoy themselves so much. Before too long, her Mom made her way over to where she and Frank were standing.

"Well, what did you think of our big news?" she asked, smiling from ear to ear.

"I don't mean to rain on your parade Mom, but we don't really understand what the big deal is."

"Yeah, I mean we get it, that it's kind of important, that the farm is paid for I guess," Frank said.

"I think you two will be able to appreciate just how important this is, when you have families of your own, someday. Anyway, this is a big tradition around here. Your Father has worked so very hard to make this happen and at such a young age. You two should be proud of him," Margaret said.

"We are Mom. We know that Dad's as hard a worker as there is," Abby said.

"Yeah, what she said," Frank chimed in.

"It sounds like there is a but in there, somewhere," Margaret said.

"Never mind, it isn't important," Abby said.

"You two make sure you tell your Dad that you're proud of him, when you see him."

"We will Mom," Abby said.

Abby remembered that day like it was yesterday. She wanted to tell her Mom that she didn't care about any of that. She was fifteen. All that she cared about was that her Father was never around when she was growing up. She should have told him how she felt, and now she would never get the chance.

●　　●　　●　　●　　●

She didn't think that Billy was a bad guy. Everyone in town seemed to adore him and her Dad definitely did. He couldn't fool an entire town, could he? No, her beef wasn't with Billy at all, it was with her Dad. Sometimes she thought, that he loved the farm more than her and Frank. She wiped the tears from her eyes and sat at the side of the road, thinking back again, to the night of the party.

"You enjoying the party sweetheart?" Dad asked her.

"Yeah, the food was amazing. I'm so stuffed, I couldn't eat another bite."

"That's good, glad to hear. You know what this means don't you? This means that I won't have to work so hard and I can spend it with you guys. That's why this night is so important to me. All I ever wanted, was to provide a good home for your Mom and you kids. It was never about the money, never. I'm sorry I haven't been around as much as I should have, but that's all about to change. I love you all very much."

"I love you too, Dad," she said, and gave him the biggest hug ever.

"Now where's your brother? I want to tell him the same thing."

Abby pointed to the other side of the room, where Frank was talking to their cousin Johnny.

"Thanks," he said, winking at her and setting off in Frank's direction.

Abby knew that her Dad meant every word of what he said that night, but that didn't change anything.

In the weeks and months following the party, her Dad made a concerted effort to be more present. Abby and Frank weren't always home now, though. They were teenagers after all, and Abby had finally made a few friends that she started hanging around with. Her Dad had been absent for so long that it was awkward when they did try to connect. They really didn't know each other all that well. Her Mom told her to be patient and keep trying, but it seemed like she was being pulled in many directions. She got a part time job in town, so that took up some of her time and before she knew it, she saw her Dad in passing only, just like before. It seemed almost better that way, it wasn't as weird and awkward. It was just easier to go back to living the way that they had become accustomed to. It seemed like a good idea to try to build a relationship with her Father, but in reality, it just never worked out.

Abby continued sitting at the side of the road thinking for several more minutes before driving off. She had wasted too much time already and she had to get back, to get ready for the funeral.

Billy had finished saying his goodbyes to the farm and now he was ready to go say his goodbyes to his Father. He went to the house, where Frank was still sitting at the kitchen table, with an empty glass in his hand. Abby was still nowhere to be seen.

"At least I didn't finish the whole bottle," Frank said, holding up the bottle for Billy to see.

He was clearly drunk, and Billy helped him to the couch to lay down.

Billy wanted to make himself scarce before Abby returned. She was going to be pissed when she saw what had become of Frank. He had a quick shower and then went to his room to get ready. He put on his new suit, that he had bought for the occasion and then read over the speech that he had re-written the night before. He could hear Frank and Abby talking in the other room. It sounded like they were crying instead of arguing. In either case, Billy wanted to avoid the whole situation. He crept down the hall and carefully opened and closed the door without making a sound. Once outside, he was able to relax a bit. He jumped into his truck and headed for town. He was supposed to pick Lisa up at 1 o'clock and he was an hour early, but he wanted to see if she would go for lunch with him before the funeral. He was hungry for one thing, but he really just wanted to get out of the house, and avoid Abby.

Lisa wasn't ready when he arrived, but she quickly put a few things away, and they went out for lunch.

"How you doing? Hanging in there?" Lisa asked.

"I spent some time walking around the farm, just kind of saying my goodbyes, you know? That might sound a little weird I guess, but the farm is more than just dirt and trees to me," Billy said.

"That doesn't sound strange to me at all. Those of us who have lived here all of our lives, understand. The country gets into your blood, and those that are lucky enough to have farms, know how it can get into your soul," Lisa said.

"Pretty deep stuff," Billy said, laughing.

She responded by punching him in the shoulder, playfully.

"I think you would have a hard time convincing Frank and Abby of that," Billy said.

"Some people just don't get it."

"Yeah, I guess I was one of those people before I came."

"Well, I'm sure glad that you found your way here," Lisa said.

"Me too. So, are you hungry? I'm starving."

"I could eat."

.   .   .   .   .

After they were done eating they made their way to the church where Billy dropped Lisa off, and continued to the funeral home.

"I feel bad dropping you off like this but the viewing at the funeral home is for family only," Billy said, glumly.

"It's okay, really. You shouldn't give it another thought. You have more important things to think about right now. It's a nice day, I'll just go sit in the park across the road."

The truth was that he wished that she could come with him, not because he felt bad, but because he could use a friendly face and someone to lean on. In any case, that wasn't going to be. He just had to go this one alone.

Abby and Frank were already at the funeral home when he got there, as well as several other people that he wasn't familiar with. They were busy talking and so he slipped past them without incident.

He signed the guest book and made his way slowly into the room where Jacob was. Billy thought again about how good it would have been to have Lisa here to lean on. His thoughts drifted to Henry's funeral and how much of a basket case he had been on that day. Looking back now, he couldn't believe that he made it through it. He thought, that if he could make it past that, then surely, he could make do today.

There was a table set up with pictures on it. Abby must have done it when she came into town, earlier. There were pictures of the four of them and some with just Jacob and Margaret. Some were of Jacob when he was younger, with his Mom, Dad and sister. The one on the end caught Billy's attention. There was a picture of Jacob kneeling beside a for sale sign, with sold written across it, out in front of the farmhouse. He was smiling from ear to ear. Written at the bottom in scrawling cursive was: The second love of Dad's life. Billy assumed that whomever had written it meant that Margaret was his first, and he thought that was a fairly safe assumption.

Billy had come to the end of the line. He was standing only feet away from Jacob's casket now. He hadn't looked up yet and he was trying to gather his courage, to do just that.

"He looks so peaceful. He's with his beloved Margaret now. We should be happy for him. I know we are all sad that we won't be spending any more time with Jacob, but we all have so many good memories of him and those will get us through. Time heals all wounds, he would say," the reverend said, as he guided Billy toward the casket.

"I've said my goodbyes. I'll leave you two alone. God bless," he said and turned and walked away.

"Thank you reverend," Billy said quietly, but he had already crossed the room.

Billy lifted his eyes and there was Jacob, wearing the new suit that he had picked, for this very occasion. He did look peaceful, content even, and that did make Billy feel more at ease.

"I love you Dad and I miss you. I wanted you to know, that I met a nice girl from town, just like you wanted me to. She's pretty cool. Her name is Lisa. I felt so all alone when you left, but I don't feel like that anymore. I don't have any experience with girls, but I still think that she may be the one. I'm going to be leaving soon, but I promise I'll come back to visit, occasionally. Thank you for being there for me, for just being you. I love you," Billy said, and laid his head on Jacob's chest.

Billy stayed that way for a minute. He straightened up, then smoothed out Jacob's suit. He stood looking at him for a few seconds and then turned and walked across the room, and out the door.

Frank and Abby watched Billy pay his respects from afar and let him have his time with their Father, without interfering.

Billy found that it was easier saying good bye to Jacob, than he could have imagined. There were several reasons for that however. He was expecting to have some trouble with Abby and was happy that it never happened. He guessed, that even Abby knew better than to cause a scene, at her Father's funeral. Billy had for the most part said his goodbyes on the night that Jacob had died and so today was just a formality. He hoped that Jacob was reunited with Margaret. He knew that Jacob was counting on that happening when he passed and so he never feared death, but Billy still wasn't sure what he believed yet.

All he knew for sure was that he wanted to see Lisa again and so he drove to the church and then went into the park to find her. She was the main reason for him finding it easier, to say goodbye to Jacob. He had someone else in his life now. They had only just met, but he felt that she was someone that he could fall in love with.

CHAPTER EIGHTEEN

He found Lisa sitting on a bench watching an older gentleman playing catch with his dog.

"Is this seat taken?" Billy asked, from behind her.

Lisa spun her head around to face him. "That was quick. Are you alright? How'd it go?" she asked.

"Actually, better than expected. Abby and Frank gave me my space, and I said goodbye to Dad on my own terms. To be honest I had already said my goodbyes the night he died. I spent some time with him before the coroner came and took him away. Well, yesterday helped as well. You helped more than you could know, thank you," Billy said.

"Just glad I could help. I like you Billy, you seem like a kind soul."

There she was doing it again. It made him squeamish when she talked like that. It was like she was setting the bar higher than he could ever achieve, setting him up to fail. But then again, it really wasn't her doing it. It was his own insecurities, getting the best of him again. He was able to keep it at bay for Jacob and he saw no real reason, that he couldn't do it for her as well.

"We have a few minutes before we have to go in. Do you want to rehearse your speech?"

"No, I think getting through it once will be hard enough. Thanks though. I'd rather just spend some quiet time with you, if that's okay?" Billy said.

"That's absolutely fine with me," she said, grabbing his hand in hers and putting her head on his shoulder.

They sat without talking. It felt so comfortable being with her. It was something he could really get used to.

"Shit! We have to go!" Billy said, looking at his watch.

Lisa jumped a bit, at the sudden break in the silence.

"Sorry, look at the time," Billy said, turning his watch toward her.

"I guess so," she said, jumping to her feet. "Let's go," she said, running toward the church, with Billy following right beside her.

People were still milling about the church, awaiting the arrival of the hearse bearing Jacob in it. Because Jacob hadn't gotten the chance to update his will, Billy was excluded from being a pall-bearer. That honour fell to Frank, three of Jacob's life-long friends, his brother James and his cousin Gene.

Billy and Lisa went inside and sat in the second row of pews, at the other end, away from where Abby and Frank were sitting. They were busy whispering to one another and didn't even notice them come in. The rest of the people found their seats and the service began. It was the normal church rhetoric, which Billy had no use for. They sang songs and read psalms, readings from the bible and the reverend assured everyone of everlasting life if they believed in Jesus, blah, blah, blah. Billy still wasn't right with God, but he knew that if he ever was, it would be on his own terms and not in a church, full of traditions and mindless followings.

He didn't hear much of what they said anyway. He was too busy thinking of Jacob.

Lisa jabbed him in the ribs. Billy spun his head to look at her.

"They're calling for you to read, followed by Abby and Frank. Good luck," she whispered.

Billy got to his feet, and made his way slowly to the podium, his speech clutched tightly in his right fist.

He paused for a minute to look over the crowd. So many familiar faces looking back at him, that had made him feel so welcome in their small town. He opened his speech and lay it on the podium before him and then began to speak.

"I look out over the crowd and I see so many kind faces. I'm glad that you are all here to share in the celebration of Jacob's life and I know, that there is no place that any of us, would rather be. I'm going to be honest, I wasn't sure what to say. I wasn't sure that any words I wrote, would do justice to my Dad."

Abby let out a bit of a snort from the front row and Billy paused to gather himself, before continuing.

"I, along with everyone here, knows that Jacob was not my biological Father, obviously, but he was a better Dad to me than my own, by a long shot. He accepted me for who I was and he always made me feel special and loved. He was my very best friend, teacher and mentor and I loved him so very much. I came into his life when he needed me and I needed him. He taught me how to grieve after the death of my brother and I think I helped him, by letting him tell me stories of his beloved Margaret."

Someone from the back yelled, "His favourite subject," and there was a murmur of laughter, that spread quickly through the crowd.

"I hope more than anything, that Dad is with Margaret right now. I know, that is what kept him going. The belief, that when he died, they would be re-united. So, I know we are sad that we won't be seeing him anymore, but I know that he didn't fear death, because he looked forward to seeing her again. I had written a different speech, but yesterday I changed this portion of it. I was walking around the farm yesterday, saying my goodbyes to the farm and to Dad and something occurred to me that hadn't before. I believe, that moments such as these are important, to remember the lives of those that we have lost, but also, to teach those of us that are still living. My Father, my real Father I mean, was not a very good Dad to me. He's not a bad man or a mean man, he just lost his way. Jacob was an amazing Dad to me and I am so thankful that he came into my life, but I think that timing is everything. I know that Dad thought of Margaret and his kids, every, single day of his life. I know that he wanted to see his children and grandchildren more, but I think deep down he understood why he didn't. When I met Dad, he was retired from farming and he needed help with the farm, and that's where I came in. When he was younger he worked so hard to provide for his family, that he didn't have the time to spend with them, that he did with me. I know that he regretted that part of his life, every day. I know that he would have done anything, to change that. Sometimes in life, we don't see things until after the moment has passed and we have time to reflect. I want to celebrate the life of Jacob and let's not dwell on any mistakes that he might have made. Let us all think for a minute of his kind smile, his warm heart and his positive outlook and remember that all wounds heal with time. Can we take a minute to remember Jacob, please?" Billy concluded, bowing his head in silence.

He closed his eyes and with the rest of the congregation remembered good times with Jacob. He smiled contentedly and then opened his eyes. There standing in front of him was Abby. She took a step closer, then paused. He had to restrain himself from taking a step backward. Surely, she wouldn't start anything, in front of the entire congregation. Billy stepped back from the podium, to allow Abby access, but she didn't go to the podium. Instead, she side-stepped in the same direction that he did. Billy looked at her for the first time, really looked at her. She was crying steadily as she took another step toward him. She held out her arms and enveloped him in a tight hug. Billy stood with his arms at his sides. He was confused and didn't know what to do, but he knew that he certainly didn't want to hug her back.

"Thank you Billy, for that beautiful speech. I understand now, I really do. I did earlier, but your speech just confirmed what I was already thinking. Thank you," she said, through tears and sobs.

Billy reluctantly hugged her back, and responded simply. "You're welcome."

Abby let go of him and went to the podium and Billy returned to his seat. Lisa looked over at him and raised her eyebrows, as if to say, "what was that?"

Billy shrugged, and mouthed the words. "I'll tell you after."

Billy understood more, after Abby's speech.

"I was thinking earlier, about the party that my parents hosted, when they paid off the farm. I know that many of you were there, and it's good to see you all again, although I wish it were under different circumstances. That was such a pivotal time in our lives as a family, unfortunately, none of us realized just how important it was, at the time. I never understood, until today. I have finally been able to let go of the resentment toward my Father and I get it now, much of what Billy was saying. The timing was just off, but I know that our Father, did love us very much. The thing that I regret the most, is not being able to tell Dad now that I love him, and to make him more of a priority in my life."

It was at that point, that emotion overtook her and she was unable to continue. Frank went up on to the stage and simply said, "thank you to everyone for coming," and then helped Abby to her seat.

The reverend concluded the service and then the immediate family and Lisa went to the cemetery for the internment ceremony, then back to the basement of the church, for sandwiches and drinks.

"No need to explain. I get what happened," Lisa said, afterwards.

"It sure surprised the heck out of me. I thought at first, she was going to cause a scene. I couldn't believe when she hugged me," Billy said.

"I was a little worried at first, to be honest. That was a very nice speech, Billy. I think you paid tribute to Jacob very nicely, while at the same time, trying to give Frank and Abby some peace in the process. You know what else I think?"

"What's that?"

"I think you are an amazing person, and I think I'd like to get to know you better. If that's alright with you?" Lisa said.

"I can't think of anything that would please me more," Billy said.

He thought briefly about the trouble that plagued him, but that was a thing of the past, hopefully forever.

Billy and Lisa visited with all the guests at the luncheon; sometimes together and sometimes on their own. Billy saw Frank and Abby at various times, but they never approached him, and he never made a point of going to talk to them.

Abby did come to see him, just as he was about to leave.

"So, we'll see you at the farm later then. I don't have to get back until tomorrow. I'd like to sit and talk with you for a bit, if that's okay?"

"That would be fine. I'll see you later then," Billy said.

"I wonder what that's about," Lisa said, when they were outside.

"I think she wants to clear the air. All this time I thought that she was the biggest bitch on the planet, and now I think that she was just hurting, that's all."

"Wow! After the way that she has been acting? I'm not so sure that I'd be so understanding."

"Let's just say, I have some experience on the subject."

"Can you drop me off at home, before you go out to the farm please? I have some things to do. Call me later?" Lisa asked.

"Sure, no problem."

Billy dropped her off at home and then drove to the farm. He was wondering what it was that Abby had to say. He pulled into the driveway and parked his truck. He felt more at ease here now, then he had since Abby had arrived. He found it amazing how his perspective had changed. It was easy to sit back and think about it after the fact, but the true strength of character is recognizing it at the time. That was something Billy certainly hadn't mastered yet. That was something that evidently Jacob hadn't either, until he was much older. Billy had a lot of respect for Jacob and this new revelation did nothing to change his opinion of him. He guessed that the old adage, that nobody's perfect, still rang true.

He went to the refrigerator and got himself a nice cold beer and went out onto the stoop to sit and relax. Minutes later Frank and Abby returned from town. Abby sat down in the chair beside him and Frank went inside to get a couple of drinks. Frank returned shortly after, handed one to Abby and then sat in the chair across from her.

Abby turned in her chair so that she was facing Billy.

"Let me start by saying, I'm sorry Billy. I'm sorry for the way that I treated you, and for the mean things that I said. Earlier today after Frank and I got in an argument, I went for a drive to clear my head and that's when I started to make sense of this whole mess. I was jealous of the relationship that you had with our Father. I know that Dad loved us very much, but it always seemed like the timing was just off with us. Your speech brought it all full circle for me, and I realized that we are all just victims of circumstance. Well, that and sometimes we need to take our heads out of our asses and not be so stubborn. I regret not having this conversation with my Dad, but I never saw it for what it was until today. Kind of an epiphany of sorts you could say," she said, and folded her hands on her lap and awaited Billy's response.

"I accept your apology. I must say, it seems surreal to me, to be having a civilized conversation with you. I had an 'ah hah' moment last night as well. Before that, I never questioned why or what, made you behave the way you did. I just knew that I didn't like the way you talked to me, or your actions, but then I realized that most times, people have an underlying reason to behaving as they do. That's when I started to think about how timing, while it isn't everything like some people say, it sure has a huge impact in our lives," Billy said.

"I'm so happy that we cleared the air. I know Dad would have been pleased as well. So, I've been talking with Frank, and we think that we came up with a fair proposal for you. Dad hadn't changed his will yet, as you are well aware of, and even though the law says that everything belongs to Frank and me, we know that Dad wanted you to have the farm and the truck. We think that if we would have been able to talk to Dad, then things may have been different. I know that's easy to say after the fact," Abby said.

"No, I agree. A lot of things were left unsaid by you two, and by Dad. I think he would have changed his mind, given these new set of circumstances,"

"How old are you? You seem far too wise, for your young age," Abby said.

"I've encountered a lot in my life so far and I attribute a lot to Dad. We used to sit right here and talk for hours. He taught me a lot in the time that we spent together."

"I can't recall ever having a full conversation with my Father," Abby said quietly, sadly.

"Anyway, we were thinking that you could stay on and run the farm. You'd have a place to live and we could pay you a small wage on top. Abby and I would split the profits from the farm, and of course we would change the ownership of the truck over to you," Frank said.

"That's an interesting proposal. I had resigned myself to the fact, that I was going to be moving on. I don't know what to say," Billy said.

"Just think about it. I have to go back tonight but Abby will be here until the morning. Whatever you two decide is fine with me. We would like to try and respect Dad's wishes as best we can," Frank said.

"Well, you've certainly given me something to think about."

"Maybe we can talk over breakfast, before I head back," Abby said.

"That would be good," Billy said.

"Now, if you would excuse me I'm worn out. I think I'm going to lie down," she said.

"Are you okay?" Frank asked.

"Yes, fine, just tired."

Abby left and went to lie down. Frank and Billy sat and had a couple of beers together, before he had to head back home.

"I'm glad we had a chance to get to know each other a little bit. I can see why Dad liked you so much," Frank said.

"That's nice of you to say. I'm glad too. I think Dad would have been really happy that we were getting along," Billy said.

"Yeah. Both Abby and I have a different view of our Father now, thanks to you. Thank you for that," Frank said, and hugged him.

"You're welcome, but I think Dad can take the credit for that. He is a constant voice in my head, now," Billy said.

Frank laughed and then went into the house to get his suit case, got in his car and left for home. Billy was left on the stoop with only his thoughts, once again. It was sure funny, how much things had changed in one day. He sat thinking, about what Abby and Frank had proposed, and the first thing he thought about, was telling Lisa. What a difference a day can make, he thought again.

CHAPTER NINETEEN

It was getting dark again. Billy had never been as thirsty in his life as he was right now. He could deal with the pain, the nausea and his splitting headache, but the thirst threatened to drive him mad. He scraped enough snow together, to quench his thirst, ever so slightly, and the burning in the back of his throat subsided for the time being.

He had made peace in his mind with Henry, his Dad and Jacob but he still had some work to do where Lisa and God were concerned.

He wished that he had a second chance to make it right with Lisa. He couldn't imagine what she must have thought, what she must be thinking now. How could he be so selfish? The answer to that question was complex. It really wasn't him, was it? No, it was the hollowness once again. Billy may have lived a much different life, had it not been for the hollowness. No matter how long he held it at bay, it always returned, stronger and more malevolent then before.

He continued thinking about Lisa. God would have to wait his turn.

CHAPTER TWENTY

The next morning Billy wanted very badly to go into town to see Lisa but he was supposed to have breakfast with Abby. Why not kill two birds with one stone? he thought. Lisa was working anyway, so he invited Abby to join him at the diner for breakfast. It was on her way home and he would get to see Lisa, it was a win- win.

Lisa was happy to see him, but she was very surprised to see that Abby was with him.

"Good morning. I don't believe we've met. I saw you at Dad's funeral, but I never got the chance to talk to you."

"Yes, I wouldn't have missed it for anything. Jacob was awesome. Oh, I'm sorry. I guess I don't need to tell you what he was like. I'm very sorry for your loss," Lisa said.

"That's okay, I know what you mean. It seems everyone knew how great he was except Frank and me," she said sadly.

"I didn't mean anything by it, I'm sorry," Lisa said.

"No, no, it's not you, it's me," Abby said, reaching out her hand, and touching Lisa lightly on the arm.

"Alright then, can I get you something to drink?" she said, changing the subject to something more familiar to her.

They ordered their coffees, their breakfast and Lisa had time to stay and chat for a while.

"So how long have you two been seeing each other?" Abby asked.

"For the last two and a half years," Lisa said, laughing.

"Just recently," Billy said.

"I've had my eye on him since he came to town, but sadly he never noticed me," Lisa said, feigning major disappointment.

"I see. Well, you two make a cute couple," Abby said.

"Well thank you. I agree," Lisa said, and went to wait on another customer.

"I like her. She seems nice. So, have you given any thought to what we talked about last night?" Abby asked.

"I've given it a lot of thought as a matter of fact, but I want to talk to Lisa about it, before I make a decision. Can I call you and let you know what I decide?"

"Yeah sure, that's fine. Take your time, there's no hurry," Abby said.

Abby left, Billy said bye to Lisa and then went back to the farm and waited for her to finish work.

It was such a different feeling being back at the farm. The last time he was there alone it was under such different circumstances. He had resigned himself to the fact that he was leaving and he had hopes of going away with Lisa. She said that she had plans to leave soon anyway, so it wasn't like she would be leaving for him. The question was, how willing would she be to stay?

Lisa drove out to the farm after supper and Billy showed her around the place, before he told her what Abby and Frank had proposed. Lisa loved the place, as he had hoped that she would.

"So, I assume you're going to take the deal. It seems like everyone gets what they want that way. They get money coming in and you get to stay on the farm and earn a little money to boot. It seems like a good partnership to me," Lisa said.

"Yeah, absolutely, I agree. It's just that I was wondering, what your plans are. I know you were planning to leave as soon as you got some money saved," Billy said.

"Yeah for sure. I was planning to leave, hopefully within the next three months. I guess that gives me three months to find out, if there's a reason for me to stay," she said coyly.

"That's too long, you'll be sick of me by then," Billy said.

"I guess we'll just have to wait and see how it goes then, won't we?" she said, kissing him and then skipping ahead.

That's exactly what they did and it went very well. Since that first day that they went to the ocean and jumped off the cliff together, they had been inseparable. They tried to take it slowly, because Lisa had been through a couple of bad relationships and this was Billy's first, but Lisa spent as much time at the farm as she did at her apartment, maybe more. They were very mindful of taking things slowly, but it was harder said than done.

Lisa was instrumental in helping Billy face his demons. She reminded him very much of Jacob that way. He told her what had happened with Henry. He left out the part about the hollowness, but he told her that he had pushed him and that's why he fell. Billy told her about his Mom's death and about how hard it had been on his Dad. With Lisa's help and probably a little of Jacob's help too, he was able to understand how lost his Father was. She encouraged him to reach out to him and try to reconcile. Billy understood now that it was circumstances more than anything else, that made his Father who he was. He understood much more, after seeing how affected Frank and Abby were by circumstance, or timing. Call it what you want, but it still amounted to the same thing.

Lisa could get Billy to talk about stuff, that he never thought that he would ever tell another living soul. She didn't have to drag these things out of him either. He genuinely wanted to tell her about himself, it was a liberating experience for him.

"I know how incredibly difficult that it can be to talk about our demons, or skeletons in our closets if you want to call them that. I'm proud of you for being able to go so far out of your comfort zone."

"I have you and Jacob to thank for that. I would never have been able to open up so much, before," he said.

"I remember our first date. You wouldn't say boo at first, but on the way home, you talked my ear off."

"You made me feel comfortable right from the start. These last few months with you have been exactly what I needed. When Jacob died, I thought, that would be the end of my happiness. I was wrong, it was only a new beginning."

"Aww, that's so sweet. I feel like we make a good team. I hope you know, that there is nothing that you can't tell me. I feel like I can be completely open and honest with you, and I know that you feel the same way. I love you Billy," she said

"And, I love you," Billy said.

Thoughts of Lisa moving or running away were things of the past.

CHAPTER TWENTY-ONE

It was just before Christmas that they decided to make the drive to Billy's home town, to visit his Father. Billy had demons that he needed to face, more than Lisa knew. There were just some things that he had to keep from her, that he couldn't share.

"You know, you're going to have to deal with your past, before you can move forward, right? Someday, if we're still together and we wanted to have kids, you would have had to deal with your feelings toward your own Father, before you could be the best Father to our kids that you could possibly be," she said.

"I agree. I don't think that I would have come to that conclusion without you, but I do agree. I'm sure I could have found a million reasons to keep putting it off. It might have gotten to the point, that I never would have found the right time. I can certainly understand now, how things could have gotten the way they had between Abby, Frank and Jacob," Billy said.

Billy figured that he would find his Father at the local pub and that's exactly where he was. It was just after quitting time and he always stopped off for a drink before he went home. Billy and Henry spent a lot of time here as kids, watching their Father drink himself into oblivion. It was fair to say that Bill had a lot of demons himself, and Billy knew, that one visit wasn't going to save anyone. He did know that it would help him to close this chapter of his life and that he could then move forward.

Lisa and Billy entered through the side door and grabbed a booth in the back.

"I think I should talk to him first and then I'll introduce the two of you, if everything goes alright," Billy said quietly, almost whispering.

"If that's the way you want it Billy, but I think that it might be better if we go together. He might be easier to talk to, with me there. He may not want to cause a scene in front of me."

"You may be right. I'm ready if you are?" Billy half said, half asked.

"Right beside you Billy. Lead the way."

They walked through the bar and Billy guided Lisa around a few tables until they came to the side wall away from the bar. Billy wondered if she might think he had chickened out, but he could tell from her reaction, that she quickly understood what he was up to.

"I don't want to sneak up on him. I want him to see us coming," Billy said.

"Yeah, I figured it out."

Billy pursed his lips, raised his eyebrows and gave her his best bobble head impression, as if to say, "look who thinks she's so smart."

Bill, did in fact see them coming and his reaction was different than anything Billy could have imagined. He turned in his bar stool and faced them, eagerly waiting for them to close the distance, a huge smile on his face.

"Wow this is a surprise! Come on, let's grab a booth so we can catch up," Bill said.

He took off, toward the end of the room to where the booths were. Billy looked at Lisa and shrugged his shoulders, grabbed her hand and followed his Father. He couldn't remember ever seeing his Father smile before. If he had, it was no more than a handful of times.

Bill slid into his seat and motioned for Billy and Lisa to follow suit. They removed their coats and then slid into the booth across from him.

"First things first, who is this beautiful young lady?" he asked.

"Lisa, meet my Father, Bill," Billy said.

"Pleased to meet you," Bill said, shaking her hand and smiling.

Billy was thinking. Okay what have you done with my Dad? It looked like him, but he sure wasn't acting like the miserable drunk, that he remembered from his childhood.

"Very pleased to meet you as well," Lisa said.

"So, where ya been? What you been up to?" Bill said, smiling.

"What the fuck! I've been gone for three years and you act like nothing happened and you're smiling like a fucking Cheshire cat. What the fuck!"

Lisa's eyes were wide with surprise. She had never heard Billy swear like that before and she couldn't believe his reaction.

"Billy!" she said.

"It's okay, I deserve everything I get," Bill said to Lisa.

He turned to Billy and said. "I'm not trying to pretend like nothing happened, Billy. I'm well aware of everything, and I'm not too happy with the way things were. I've thought about it nearly every minute of every day since you've been gone. I missed your brother so much that I didn't see that I still had a son standing right in front of me. At first, when you left, I thought you were better off without me. I was a hollow man and I needed to be filled up. So, I found God again. Once I got my life turned around, I wanted to re-connect with you, but I didn't know where to find you. I hoped that someday you would return," Bill said, crying a little as he spoke.

The hairs on the back of his neck were standing on end. Billy didn't hear the last of what his Dad had said. Everything he had said after, he was a hollow man and needed filling up, was lost on him. He continued to play the words over in his mind. He tried to look cool so that Lisa wouldn't suspect anything, but it was a difficult thing to do.

"Billy?" Lisa said.

"Yeah, what?" Billy responded.

"You drifted off there. Are you alright?" she whispered in his ear. "I think he's trying really hard here. You could meet him half way."

Billy thought about all the times that he and Henry were left alone at home to fend for themselves. Billy was still a kid himself, and it wasn't fair what his Dad did to them. He was supposed to be the adult. They just wanted to be kids.

"I can appreciate that, but Henry and I had a really shitty go of it, you know?" Billy said, and got up from the table and went to the bathroom, to cool off.

He splashed his face, hoping that the cool water would clear his thoughts. I was a hollow man, I needed filling up, echoed over and over in his mind. There were a lot of things that he wanted to say to his Father, that he needed to answer for, but Billy could only think of what he was just told..

He stayed in the bathroom until he could collect his thoughts a little. He looked in the mirror and he saw himself looking back at him, but there was someone else there, wasn't there? Someone that had been there all the while, but until this very moment, had gone unnoticed. He was there just below the surface, hidden behind his tanned face and gentle eyes. He had been there his whole life and he had never known it. Now he understood. He understood everything.

He wiped his face with a paper towel and went back out and sat down with Lisa and his Dad.

"Are you okay? You were in there a long time," Lisa asked.

"I'm fine, at least I am now," Billy said.

He knew that this was not the time nor the place to have the conversation with his Dad, that he needed to have. He would have to be content to hear him out and then sometime in the future, he would have the conversation that he really wanted to have; when Lisa wasn't there.

Bill told their story from start to finish. It was a story that Lisa had heard before, but from Billy's point of view. The story of his wife dying and how he was ill-equipped to deal with it. He talked about how great a Father his Dad had been to him and how he felt inadequate as a Father himself. He apologized many times for his shortcomings, during his tale, for being weak and not being there for his kids, when they needed him the most. He knew that he didn't deserve it, but he wanted to be a part of their lives and to try and make amends. He said that he was a different man than he was. He had made his peace with God and that had changed everything.

"You say you've changed, and yet here you are at the bar, right where I knew I would find you," Billy said, clearly disgusted.

"I don't drink any more Billy. Here, taste for yourself," he said, holding it out for Billy to taste.

Billy grabbed it and held the glass under his nose to smell. There was no smell of alcohol but he tasted it anyway. Sure enough, it was only cola.

"Then why do you come to the bar then?" Billy asked.

"These people are about as close to friends as I have. I've spent so much time here over the years, that I don't know where else to go. Home is full of loneliness and bad memories and I can't stand it there," Bill said, looking down at his hands in front of him.

Now Billy felt like a heel. He reached across the table and grabbed one of his Dad's hands.

"I'm sorry. It's just that so many bad memories, and so many hard times, can't be erased in a couple of hours. It's going to take time to be able to trust, that what you're saying is true, you know? I'll have to see it for myself to believe it, that's all," Billy said.

"I understand completely, no pressure. It is good to see you Billy and to meet you Lisa."

"Well I for one am starved. Have you eaten Bill?" Lisa asked.

"Not yet, just got done work."

"How's the food here?" Lisa asked.

"It's not that bad, actually. They have a decent selection. To be honest I eat here more times than not. It's just not worth cooking a meal for just me most of the time."

The three of them had supper together, and it went better than Billy could have imagined. In fact, the entire visit went far better, then he ever thought it would. The only thing troubling him, was what his Dad had said earlier. Billy had used the same expression on many occasions and he thought it had to be more than a mere coincidence. He was biding his time, waiting to ask him about it.

He had to wonder just how similar they really were. After all he was his Father's son. He didn't realize just how much he resembled him, until earlier in the bathroom, when he looked in the mirror and saw his Dad looking back at him. Sure, Billy was much younger looking than him, but the resemblance was uncanny.

Finally, Lisa excused herself and went to the bathroom. Billy knew he didn't have a lot of time, to find out everything he wanted to know. He was hoping that he could at least find out, if his definition of the hollowness, matched his own.

"Dad, I need to ask about something you said earlier. You said something about hollowness and filling up. What did you mean by that?" Billy asked, urgently.

"I just meant, that I get a feeling that I'm not whole, not complete you know? Like there is some external force controlling me sometimes," he answered.

"No, not exactly. Can you try to explain more please?" Billy said.

Of course he had an idea what he meant, but he wanted him to say it..

"Do you ever get the feeling like there is something missing? I do all the time. It's been with me since your Mother died. Of course, I felt as though I wasn't complete, because I missed your Mother so much and I didn't know how to continue on. I filled the emptiness with booze for years, until recently, when I found God again. Now the empty feeling is gone and I feel truly alive, for the first time since your Mother passed."

"What are you guys talking about? What did I miss?" Lisa asked.

"I was just telling Billy, that finding God again, has completely turned my life around," Bill said.

"Oh," Lisa said, as if she was sorry she asked.

"You're not religious, I take it?" Bill asked.

"Let's just say, that I stopped believing in God, when I stopped believing in the Easter bunny, the Tooth fairy and Santa Claus," she said.

"Well, maybe someday we can discuss it in more detail, but for now, let's talk about other things," Bill said.

Billy laughed a little at what Lisa had said and then breathed a sigh of relief, because he was happy to avoid talking about religion. Lisa couldn't have come back at a worse time though. Bill hadn't answered Billy's question. Actually, he had, just not to his satisfaction. Perhaps he should have phrased it differently, but he didn't know how to approach the subject. He wasn't going to just come out with it and say what was really on his mind. Hey Dad listen! Do you ever have a hollow feeling? Feel like you're a puppet, being controlled by someone, or something. A feeling so deep with despair and anger that you don't know what to do. This feeling affects you so profoundly, both physically and mentally, that you don't even feel like the same person. It makes you do things and say things, that you would normally never do or say. All reason is lost when it has its grip on you, and the only way to get free from it is to feed it. It feeds on misery and death, but if you feed it, in return you get the most euphoric feeling that you could ever imagine. It lies waiting for the right time to surface. It always knows when the right time is to feed. It makes even the best person into a liar, a cheat, a bully or sometimes a murderer. So, Dad is that the hollow feeling you're talking about or is it something a little more benign.

"Billy, Billy? Where were you there for a minute? You were a million miles away," Lisa asked.

"Huh, yeah. Just lost in thought I guess."

"Anything you want to share?" Lisa asked.

"Just thinking that's all."

"Well, that was obvious. Fine don't tell us," Lisa said.

Billy knew her well enough to know, that she wasn't upset that he didn't share what he was thinking. She probably wouldn't give it another thought. If the shoe was on the other foot however, it would drive him insane wondering what she was thinking about. They were just wired differently that's all, but they did complement each other very well.

Bill and Lisa continued talking and getting to know each other, while Billy listened in. He couldn't help but think that Lisa and he were both getting to know his Dad at the same time. He knew a lot less, than a son ought to know about his Father. Billy also thought that he liked this version of his Father much better, than the one that he remembered as a kid. He couldn't help but think how different things might have been, if this was the Father that he grew up with, instead of the version that he and Henry had been stuck with. It's funny how things go. If they had had a better childhood, then maybe Henry would still be alive right now, but then he wouldn't have met Lisa, or Jacob for that matter. There's just no way of knowing how the events in his life would have turned out. Billy drifted off again thinking, while Lisa and Bill continued to talk. They talked until the bar closed. Billy occasionally joined in the conversation, but it was Bill and Lisa that did most of the talking.

"I like your Dad. He wasn't at all what I thought he would be. I guess mostly because your description of him was so different," Lisa said, when they got into the truck and started their drive home.

"He wasn't at all what I thought he would be either. I don't know what to think. That is not the same man that raised Henry and me. I can't even say that. We raised ourselves. When he was around he was miserable, drunk or both. That is a different man, that you met today."

After that, they drove in silence for quite a while before either of them spoke. They both had to process what had just happened. Lisa met a man that seemed to be pleasant and likeable, completely different than the way that Billy had described him. She liked him and she hoped that Billy would continue to pursue a relationship with him.

Billy met a man that was completely foreign to him. If he had been meeting him for the first time as Lisa had, he was sure that he would like him. As it was however, he wasn't sure how he felt. All the ghosts of the past were hard things to let go of, it would take some time, but Billy thought that it was worth exploring.

"So, you've had some time to process. What are you thinking?" Lisa asked.

"I can't believe the transformation. I mean, it was like he was a different person, you know? If Henry and I would have had that man as a Father, it would have been so much different. It reminds me so much of what Abby and Jacob's relationship was like. I'm not comparing my Dad to Jacob, just the situation, you know?"

"Yeah, I know exactly what you mean. If you would have been meeting Bill for the first time, like you met Jacob later in life, well what a difference," Lisa said.

"Yeah, makes you think," Billy said quietly.

They fell silent once again. Apparently, it did make them think, and they were both lost in thought, for the remainder of the drive home.

CHAPTER TWENTY-TWO

All the pieces seemed to be falling into place for Billy Johnson. He had re-connected with his Father and it was going well. It had been a couple of months, since that first meeting at the bar with him and Lisa and the hardest part for Billy, was trusting that his Father was who he said he was.

"Lisa?"

"In here?" she answered, from the bedroom.

"Hey, there you are. Listen, if we don't have anything planned, I'd like to go visit my Father. I want to talk to him one on one. I'm still having trust issues where he's concerned, and I think that the only way to get past it, is just to give him time to prove himself."

"I think that's an excellent idea. It's going to take time, Billy, but I think that this is only going to help you going forward. Love you, have fun."

"I'm not so sure that I would describe it as fun, but I'll try. I won't be long. Love you."

Billy thought about what he would say to his Father, for the entire drive. When he got there, he still didn't know what it was that he wanted to say. Whatever thoughts that he had organized, went out the window, the moment that he pulled up to the house. He got out of the car and leaned against the fender, looking at the small house in front of him. All the pain and heartache from years of him keeping it bottled up inside, came flowing out of him, in the form of tears. All the years of watching his Father drink himself into a stupor. All the times that he had to stay awake with Henry, when he was sick. All the times that they had to make their own meagre supper; it all came back to him. He realized just how far he had come, and how far that he still had to go.

The door opened and his Dad walked out onto the porch. Billy hastily wiped away the tears, but it was too late.

Bill walked toward him and tried to give him a hug. Billy recoiled in disgust.

"I'm so sorry, Billy. I can only imagine how hard this must be for you. If I could do it all over again, I would. I'm sorry for being a shitty Father to you and Henry. I'm sorry for not being strong enough."

Billy didn't say a word. He shook his Dad's hand and walked toward the house. He believed him. God help him, but he did. That changed very little, however. Only time would change the way he felt about his Father. Well, time and his actions, of course. He needed to prove himself and Billy could see that his Father understood that very well.

"I understand, Billy. I know it's going to take time and I'm not going to pressure you."

Billy stood in the door way, but couldn't bring himself to go in. "I think this was a mistake," he said.

"Let's go for a walk then," Bill said.

"Yeah that might work."

They walked and talked for the better part of an hour. It was more like Billy asking questions and Bill answering them. To Bill's credit, he never became defensive. He answered Billy's questions the best that he could and apologized a lot. The number one question on Billy's mind, he avoided for the time being. He waited until he got back to his car before he asked.

"When we met at the bar a while back, you mentioned a hollow feeling that you needed to fill up. What did you mean by that?"

"I thought that I answered that. After you Mom died, I felt hollow inside, like there was something missing. I tried to fill it with booze and it worked to some extent, but it laid waste to everything else that mattered in my life. Unfortunately, you boys were right in the line of fire."

"I know, but did you ever feel like it was controlling you, like you were under its spell?"

"I don't know what I felt, to be honest. I was drunk most of the time, so that I wouldn't have to feel."

Billy didn't get the answer that he was looking for, but he let it go for the time-being.

He gave his Dad a quick, unnatural hug and went back to the farm.

"So, how was it?" Lisa asked, when he returned home.

"Draining."

"I'll bet. Come cuddle with me on the couch for a bit. No talking, I promise," she said, leading him into the living room.

The next day, Billy was ready to talk about his visit with his Dad. Lisa listened, without interrupting. She had such a way of making him feel comfortable and she understood him so well. He was starting to forget what life was like, before her. She made him a better person and he could only hope, that he could be the person that she needed him to be.

"You know, I love you, right?"

"Of course I do, Billy. You tell me every day, but that's not how I know. You know how I really know? You show me everyday. Things like, you making my lunch for work, after you finish the chores. I can tell by the way you kiss me and hold me. I know, because you listen to me bitch about work and pretend that you're interested, even though, I know that you're not."

"Busted!" Billy said, and laughed.

"I couldn't be happier, Billy."

"You took the words right out of my mouth," he said, hugging her tightly.

"In time, you will be able to forgive your Father, Billy. I'm sure of it. Some day, you might be able to forgive yourself as well."

He didn't respond. He was too lost in thought, thinking about Henry.

CHAPTER TWENTY-THREE

It was the spring, late April, actually. Lisa was three months pregnant. It certainly wasn't a planned pregnancy, but Billy couldn't be happier that they were going to have a little one together. Actually, make that two. They were expecting twins. He knew that Lisa would make the best Mother in the world, she was absolutely suited for it, but he still had some reservations about being a Dad. Renewing his relationship with his Father helped, but he still had some doubts, where he was concerned. Only time would help with that. Lisa assured him that he would be a good father, but he would be lying if he said he wasn't as scared, as he was excited. He didn't know anyone with kids, and he had no real experience looking after them; so he would have to rely heavily on Lisa. Which was totally okay, because if anyone could help him through this, it was Lisa.

During this time, he started to think about renewing his relationship with God as well. He never hid anything from Lisa, but for some reason, he never told her. He knew that she didn't believe in God, so maybe that was the reason. He just wanted it to be a private thing, between God and him. He saw how embracing God, had changed his Dad's life, and he thought it was time, that he reached out to Him as well.

Billy also found out, that yes, his Father was talking about the same ailment that afflicted him from time to time. His Father didn't seem to suffer to the same extent as Billy did, but it was there all the same. Well, his Father did suffer, but it didn't cause the extreme highs and lows as it did with Billy. Bill was miserable a lot of the time. Feeding the hollowness, made it more tolerable, but he didn't get the same sense of euphoria that Billy did. All Bill could really say, was that when he turned to God, it all started to change for him. The hollowness was banished completely and he felt like a new man.

Billy thought that if it worked for his Dad, then why wouldn't it work for him. He hadn't been visited by his affliction for quite some time. In fact, he could only remember twice that it had showed up, in all the time since he had come to this town. That being said, he didn't want to take any chances, with twins on the way and a beautiful girl that loved him, he thought that he might do all that he could, to make sure that his perfect life, continued to be just that, perfect.

·　　·　　·　　·　　·

It had rained more in the last few weeks, than Billy could ever remember. He wanted to get the tractor into the field, to start working the land, but it was far too wet for that. There were days on end, of grey, drizzly days and others that produced severe thunderstorms, with heavy rains and hail mixed in for good measure. High winds accompanied the thunderstorms and there were a lot of broken tree limbs strewn about the property. Some, were small enough for him to drag back to the bush by hand, others were too big and he would have to wait until he could get the tractor into the field.

"I don't think that it's ever going to stop raining," Billy said.

"Well, I don't have to work today, and it looks like you can't, so we might as well go back to bed," Lisa said, removing her nightie and letting it fall to the floor.

Billy scooped her in his arms and ran down the hall and into the bedroom. He laid her gently on the bed.

"I'm not made of glass you know," she said, kicking the covers off the bed.

"I know, it's just that… you're pregnant."

"I am," she said, feeling her belly, feigning surprise and laughing.

"You know what I meant."

She sat up and helped Bill remove his shirt and then his pants. She grabbed him and pulled him onto the bed beside her. They made love and then talked for a while, before making love again. At one point Lisa fell asleep and Billy lay beside her, listening to the sound of her breathing and caressing her belly with his fingers. He kissed her belly, but he was also kissing his babies.

"You are going to make a great Dad," Lisa said.

"Hmm, I thought you were sleeping."

"I was," she said, kissing him.

Billy held her in his arms and continued to caress her belly.

"Nothing I would love more, than to lie here all day with you, but I have to check how much rain we've had."

"Fine, I'll be waiting, all cold, lonely, afraid and naked, until you return," she said, covering herself with a blanket.

There were large puddles of water gathered in all the low spots and the pond was filled to the brim and beyond. If it didn't stop raining soon, it was going to start flooding up toward the house and then they might be in trouble. The spillway exiting the pond was clear for now, but occasionally debris got caught in the grate that covered the opening and Billy had to remove it. It wasn't a big job normally, when the water was lower, but the way the water was flowing at the moment, it would be, soon.

Billy went back to the house, after he was satisfied that the spillway was still clear. Four hours later he went to check it again, just to be sure. He opened the door and stood on the stoop. A howling wind out of the west, was driving rain up onto the stoop and the entire porch was covered in water. It was a good seven feet to the edge of the roof and Billy had never seen water make it more than a couple of inches up the porch. Usually the roof protected it, but this was not an ordinary day. Billy took a couple of steps forward and noticed that the water in the yard had crept another fifteen feet toward the house. He couldn't believe what he was seeing. It meant that the spillway was probably plugged and like it or not, he was going to have to unplug it. Lisa came out of the house and stood next to him. She didn't need to be told what was wrong or what Billy intended to do next.

"Billy Johnson, I know what you're thinking, and you're not going out in the worst storm that I have ever seen."

"I have to. If I don't, the water is going to be up to the house in a half an hour and then it's going to leak into the basement and we'll have a hell of a mess on our hands."

"There must be someone that we can call, to come and help," Lisa said.

"It's fine, really. I probably just have to clear a couple of branches and then it'll be alright. It's only water, a lot of it sure, but I'll be okay."

"Well, I'm coming. I want to make sure you don't do anything stupid. No arguments!" she said, sternly.

Billy knew better than to argue with her, once she set her mind to something, besides it was only rain, no big deal.

"Fine. We'll have to dry off and warm up when we get back to the house. Any idea how we can do that?" Billy asked, coyly.

"Billy, if you don't do anything stupid, then we can do whatever you want, when we get back inside," she said, smiling.

A huge flash of lightning lit up the sky in the distance, followed by the booming sound of thunder, that seemed to roll the length of the property and up the steps to where they stood. A tree at the end of the lane way creaked and groaned from the wind, it's canopy leaning wildly to the east. They watched as its trunk exploded from the strain, sending splinters of wood across the road and laneway. The tree came crashing down on the lawn, just missing the hydro wires.

"Are you sure about this?" Lisa asked.

"It'll be fine. Five minutes and then we'll be snuggled in bed, warm and dry. Let's go!" Billy said, and ran out into the driving rain.

He held his hand up to shield his eyes and turned to see Lisa coming down the steps to where he stood. He held out his hand and she grabbed it.

"Nice day for a walk, what do you say?"

"You sure know how to show a girl a good time," she said, laughing.

The pond was only slightly lower than where the house stood, but by the time they reached the end of the pond where the spillway was, they were in water up to their knees. Usually when it rained, even moderately, the water coming out of the spillway, was a roaring stream of white water, that left the pond and fell five feet to the creek below. The creek itself was only three feet below the pond at the moment and had swelled to four times its normal width. The water coming out of the pond was little more than a steady flow of water, maybe a foot in diameter. There were two large branches that were visible above the water line and their leaves were probably plugging the grate, that covered the spillway.

"See, no problem. All I have to do is remove those two branches and it'll probably do the trick. I can clean the rest out when it stops raining," Billy said.

"Be careful! If anything happens, I'm not going to be much help," Lisa urged.

"I will!" Billy yelled, over the latest boom of thunder.

Billy set to work clearing the branches. He positioned himself as close as he could and reached out to grab hold of the closest branch. The water was still up to his knees but he couldn't tell where the edge of the pond was. He leaned as far forward as he dared, trying to get a better hold of the branch, but slipped in the process. He fell forward and into the pond, going under the water as he did. He popped up, cleared his eyes with his hand and immediately looked to the shore where Lisa was standing. There was a worried look on her face, and a hint of anger.

"Are you alright? Billy enough! Let's get some help!" she yelled, over the sound of the driving wind and rain.

Billy scrambled up the bank and went to Lisa. He put his arms around her and kissed her.

"I'm fine, it's only water," he said, smiling.

Lisa didn't return his smile, she was in no mood for Billy's shenanigans.

"Billy enough! Let's go!" she implored.

"One more try and if I can't get it, then I'll get some help. I promise," he said, laying his head on her shoulder like a little puppy.

"You promise?" she asked, shrugging her shoulder to get his head off it.

"I promise. Don't worry, I'll be fine," Billy said, happily.

He turned back to the task at hand. He should have brought a rope to help him pull on the branch, but he was too stubborn and he pushed ahead anyway. He walked gingerly into the water feeling ahead with his one foot for the edge of the pond. He shuffled slowly forward until his left foot felt nothing. He lowered it deeper into the water and pulled it back toward him, until he found the edge of the pond. He took a step back until both feet were on solid ground. He was a couple of feet closer than he was on his first attempt. He grabbed hold of the branch and took a second to steady himself, before pulling. He leaned back and pulled. The branch moved slightly, but the spillway was still blocked. He slid his hand up the branch and grabbed closer to the water line. This time when he leaned back, the branch pulled free. Water rushed toward the partially unblocked spillway, causing Billy to lose his balance and fall into the pond once again. The first time, the spillway was still blocked and Billy was able to easily swim to safety. This time however, the rushing water dragged Billy under and slammed him hard against the grate covering the spillway. The branch that he had pulled free floated to the surface and became lodged above him. His head was partially above water but he was unable to draw a complete breath of air without swallowing water. He held his face as high as he could and took little sips of air. He knew that eventually the water level would fall enough and he would be able to free himself.

Lisa on the other hand was beside herself. She saw Billy lose his balance when he pulled the branch free, and then go under the water. That was the last she saw of him. The branch above him obstructed her view and so she would have thought that he was pinned under water.

"Billy! Billy! Billy!" she yelled at the top of her lungs.

Billy could hear her yelling but he was unable to answer her. He couldn't draw a large enough breath to yell back, so he just had to wait, and hope that everything would be okay, and that she didn't do anything stupid.

He could see Lisa make her way to the edge of the pond, much as he had earlier. She found the edge but she couldn't reach the branch closest to her. She yelled his name again, but he still couldn't answer. She was crying heavily now. The wind was still howling and a large boom of thunder rolled across the country side, once again. She paced back and forth, not knowing what to do. There was no time to run for help. By the time she made it back, he would be dead. She plugged her nose with her left hand and jumped in. The rushing water immediately dragged her downward and slammed her into the grate covering the spillway. She wasn't as lucky as Billy had been. She was facing downward with her legs flailing just below the surface of the water. Billy could feel her beside him, but there was no way she could help herself, let alone help him.

Oh no, what have you done, he thought. He reached down and grabbed hold of her hand. He realized right away that she was upside down and he panicked. He pulled as hard as he could and she moved toward him a bit but it also pulled him more under the water as he did. He tried to use the branch above him as leverage but the end of it was too flimsy to be of much use. He thought briefly about taking off his shirt and using it to plug the drain a little more to stop some of the water flow, but he was unable to remove it. It had been a minute already and he knew that Lisa was running out of time, if she hadn't already. He squeezed her hand and she squeezed it back. Good! At least he knew she was still alive.

Billy tried to pull her but she didn't move. He was in full panic mode now and he was all out of ideas. He had only one idea left and that was to pray. So, that's what he did.

He started by telling God he was sorry for the things that he had done and for turning his back on him, but he never got to finish.

The other branch that was against the spillway shifted slightly, from the rising water level, and it was just enough to let Billy raise his head above the water and take a deep breath. He grabbed the bars of the grate and pulled himself under water until he was below Lisa. He positioned himself under her shoulder and pulled himself and her up using the bars, until she was free from the grate. Next it was Billy's turn. He pulled himself up until he reached the end of the grate. Luckily one of the bars was broken off at the top and he was able to get his foot on top of it. He pushed as hard as he could with his foot and he popped free like a cork, once he was above the grate. He took a couple of quick, water filled breaths, coughed and then finally took a deep breath. He turned his head around, frantically searching for Lisa.

Lisa was lying face down at the edge of the pond. He swam as fast as he could to her side. By now, the water had retreated a few feet and the edge of the pond was now visible. Billy scrambled up, onto the grass and got to his feet. He grabbed hold of Lisa's hands, pulled her out of the water and across the grass and muck, away from the pond. Billy knelt beside her. Her lips were blue. Billy knew enough to know, that it wasn't a good sign.

"No! No! No!" he cried, and began trying to breathe into her mouth.

Billy had never been taught C.P.R. but he had a working knowledge of it, from seeing it on T.V., but he thought that it wouldn't hurt to pray while he did it.

He thought of Henry and how scared he had been on the day he died. He felt the same now. He could feel the coldness of Lisa's lips as he pressed his against hers and he could taste the salt of his tears as he cried over her. He prayed as he blew air into her mouth and he continued to pray as he pushed on her chest. He had no idea if he was doing it right, but he had to try. He switched back to blowing breaths into her mouth and then he paused for a moment. Her lips were no longer blue. At first, he thought that he had just warmed them up, but that was stupid.

The colour started to rush back into Lisa's body and she coughed a gurgling, phlegmy cough, that was the most beautiful sound that Billy had ever heard. He rolled her on to her side to remove the rest of the water from her mouth. She coughed and coughed until she was hoarse, and Billy was delighted by the sound of it.

Eventually her coughing subsided and he raised her from the ground and held on to her for dear life.

"Not so tight Billy," she whispered.

"Oh, sorry," he said, loosening his grip, but still holding her. He was smiling from ear to ear, and tears flowed steadily down his cheeks.

"I thought that I'd lost you. I love you."

"I love you too Billy, now can we get out of the rain?" she said, quietly.

"Yes, of course," he said, getting to his feet.

He set Lisa on her feet. She stood bent over for a minute and then went to straighten up. She made it part way and then bent back over at the waist. She was breathing heavily through her mouth.

"Something's wrong Billy. It hurts! It hurts!" she said.

Billy could tell how scared she was, from the tone of her voice. He bent down and scooped her into his arms and headed for the house. He started to run but Lisa pleaded for him to stop, because he was bouncing too much and she couldn't take the pain. By the time he reached the truck, blood had soaked through her pants and Billy's arms were covered in it. He set her in the front seat and kissed her on the forehead. The panicked look in her eyes, nearly broke his heart.

He ran to the house, got the keys and returned as quickly as he could, but it still felt like an eternity. He drove to town as fast as he could safely go. The roads were covered in water and large puddles lay at the sides of the road. Billy did his best to avoid most of them but a few of them grabbed the truck and pulled it toward the ditch. He slowed a little for fear of making things worse.

Billy held Lisa's hand with his free hand, whenever the road ahead was clear of puddles. He tried to calm her but she was inconsolable. She was scared and in pain and both Billy and she feared the worst. There was a lot of blood and neither of them could ignore the fact, that it was a very bad sign.

They arrived at the hospital, after what seemed like an hour, but was actually only ten minutes. Billy lifted Lisa out of the truck and carried her into the emergency room, as gently but as quickly as possible. It never even crossed his mind to shut the truck off, or to close the doors. A nurse met him part way across the floor and ushered him to a room immediately. By now Lisa was covered in blood from the waist down and Billy was covered from his chest to his knees.

She examined Lisa quickly, asked a few questions and then called for a doctor right away. She continued asking questions and took Lisa's blood pressure. Lisa was in and out of consciousness, so Billy had to answer most of them. The doctor was there within minutes and the nurse ushered Billy into another room, gave him some khaki pants and a shirt to wear and put his blood-soaked clothes in a bag for him. Then he wanted to get back in to see Lisa.

"I'm sorry Sir, but you'll just have to wait here until the doctor can assess your wife and I'll let you know how she is, as soon as I get an update. I know it's hard, but you'll just have to wait. She's in good hands. Doctor Wiebe is an excellent doctor," she said, kindly.

"I'm not leaving. I'm staying right here. I want to be close, so that I can see her as soon as she wakes up," Billy said.

"I understand. That's fine. I'll be back to check on you in a few minutes and I'll let you know as soon as I hear anything, about your wife's condition. Is there anything I can get for you before I go?" she asked.

"No thanks," Billy said, distractedly.

He sat for a couple of minutes, until he couldn't stand being idle any longer. He got up and paced back and forth across the room, going over and over in his mind, the events of the last couple of hours. If he had just listened to Lisa, they wouldn't be in the trouble they were in now and Lisa wouldn't be in there, fighting for her life. Thirty minutes, that seemed like hours passed and finally the nurse returned.

"Mr. Johnson, your wife has stabilized. She is conscious but she has lost a lot of blood. She has been sedated for now and we are continuing to monitor the babies' heartbeats. You can go in and sit with her for awhile, then we will have to ask you to leave again, while we run some more tests," she said.

"That's good news! So, she's going to be okay, and the babies too?" Billy asked, excitedly.

"I'll let you talk to the doctor; he'll be back to check on her in a bit," she said quietly.

Billy went in to see Lisa, sat in a chair beside her and held her hand. Her hair was a mess and her skin was a greyish colour. There were dark circles under both eyes. She had an I.V. in the top of one hand, monitors hooked up to her chest and abdomen, and she was the most beautiful person that he had ever seen. He put his hands over her right hand and sat quietly beside her, just looking at her.

"I'm sorry, I'm such a stubborn fool. I'm sorry that you are lying there and it isn't me. It should be me," he whispered.

He picked up her hand gently, raised it to his lips, kissed it slowly and then set it back down on the bed. He sat looking at her through blurry eyes. He was so happy that she was alive. He couldn't imagine his life without her.

"Mr. Johnson?" the doctor asked, when he entered the room.

Billy jumped at the sound of his voice. "Yes," he answered.

"Your wife has lost a lot of blood, but her vital signs are stable now, and with a lot of rest she'll be just fine," he said.

"That's great news Doc. How long will she have to stay here?" When can I take her home?" Billy asked, excitedly.

The Doctor's look became more serious and he exhaled deeply, before speaking again.

"Well that's what I need to talk to you about. Your wife is fine, that's the good news. Let's try to focus on that, okay? Now, unfortunately one of the fetuses didn't make it."

"One of the babies died?... The other one is okay? The other baby is still okay, right?" Billy blurted.

"Yes, Mr. Johnson the other baby is fine, for the time being."

"What do you mean, for the time being?" Billy asked.

He tried to focus on the fact that Lisa was alive, and that the one baby was as well. He couldn't let himself think beyond that, but then the Doctor continued what he was saying.

"Okay. I need to explain this to you. I'm very sorry that the one baby didn't make it. We are going to try to do everything to save the other. In this particular case, there could be complications that I want you to be aware of. It is possible for the one fetus to come to term and everything will be okay. When one of the twin fetuses dies, it doesn't automatically mean that the other fetus will die as well. Most times the expired fetus will be absorbed and will cause no problems to the remaining fetus. In this case, the likelihood of problems arising is increased because the fetuses were identical twins. That means that they shared the same placenta and a portion of it was ruptured, which unfortunately was the reason for all the blood and subsequent death of the one fetus. We will have to monitor the situation very carefully," he was saying, as Billy cut him off.

"So, what does all this mean? The other baby can still be okay, right?" Billy said.

"Yes, it is possible, but the chances are slimmer because they shared the same placenta. Sharing a placenta with a demised twin can lead to anemia, low blood pressure, and/or a restriction of blood flow to the living twin, which can lead to death. This also leads to neurological impairments in the surviving twin. Now, generally if this happens in the first trimester the risks are reduced and the chances of survival are better, but your wife is just past the first trimester, so I can't say for sure if the chances are better or worse. We are going to keep your wife in the hospital for a while and continue to monitor her and the baby. We'll wait and see. I would say, at the moment, that it would be more of a risk to remove the deceased fetus, than if we didn't. That's all I can really say, for now. Any questions?" the doctor, asked.

"Not right now," Billy mumbled.

"Okay, well if you think of anything, the nurse would be happy to answer any of your questions, and if she can't, I'll be back later doing my rounds and I could answer them for you then. Again, I'm sorry for the bad news. Take care," he said, and left.

Billy continued to hold Lisa's hand and he brushed her hair back from her face with the other.

"How am I going to tell you? How the Hell am I going to tell you this?" Billy thought, out loud.

Lisa stirred but her eyes remained closed. Billy hung his head and tried to think, but it was impossible. He continued to re-play the words that the Doctor had told him. They spun around and around in his mind and wouldn't stop. He had to go for a walk to clear his head, before he went crazy.

He went out into the hall but there were too many people there for his liking. He didn't want people to see him cry, so he went outside and walked across the grass. The rain had stopped for the time being, but even that made Billy more upset.

"Now you make it stop raining!" Billy yelled, to the heavens.

Billy sat down under a tree and leaned his back against it. He stared back in the direction of the hospital and thought of Lisa. He didn't know how he was going to tell her the bad news. His heart ached already, but it hurt even more at the thought of how Lisa was going to react to the bad news, that he had in store for her.

He thought of praying to God to help keep Lisa and their baby safe, but then he thought of the poor little innocent baby that was dead in Lisa's womb.

"Fuck you God! What kind of God are you anyway? If you have a beef with me than take it out on me! Don't take it out on a sweet, innocent, little baby and Lisa!" Billy yelled, at the sky.

Billy glanced quickly from side to side, making sure that nobody heard his outburst. There was an old man sitting on a bench on the other side of the lawn, but he didn't look up, so Billy figured that he didn't hear him.

He sat with his head on his chest bone. A sense of despair overtook him and he felt that he would be sick. He managed to steel himself against the nausea, closed his eyes and took a few deep breaths.

It had been so long and times so few and far between, that he almost didn't recognize it. The hollowness was growing, taking hold of him, trying to make him its prisoner once again. Billy fought back. He had to be strong for Lisa and his unborn baby. This was no time to succumb to it. Billy fought for all he was worth, managing to push it back down, deep inside him where it lived. It tried to persuade him, that this was the right time to emerge, once again. It was hard to resist. It seemed to come when he was at his weakest, but Billy resisted its murderous, insane rhetoric and he pushed it away. He replaced it with thoughts of Lisa, his babies, and how much he loved them. Eventually he could feel the strength of it ebbing, failing. It knew that it was beaten, for now.

CHAPTER TWENTY-FOUR

Twilight was now upon the mountain, and very soon it would be dark, once again. How long could he keep this up? He thought that tomorrow might be the end of it. He was tired most of the time now and he slept more than he was awake. He had an ever-present, splitting headache and he had started to lose the feeling in his toes and the tips of his fingers. He was having trouble focusing on any objects, that were more than a few feet in front of him and there was a constant ringing in both ears. His mind was playing ticks on him as well. Twice he heard Lisa calling out to him and he tried to respond, but only managed a croak from his dry throat and lips. A minute later he was cursing himself for being so stupid. Twice now, he imagined a flashlight bobbing through the trees. He thought at first that it was light from fire flies, but it was the wrong time of year for them. Between his mind playing tricks on him and his senses betraying him, he wasn't sure what was real any longer.

He saw the light shining from between the trees once again. He was amused by the fact, that he was losing his mind. He laughed a little out loud, which sent fresh stabs of pain cascading down his throat and into his lungs.

There was the light again! Could he really just be imagining it?

Again! He thought that he saw some movement with it that time. Could his eyes be playing tricks on him?

Billy swallowed, waited for the pain to subside, then tried to call out.

"Hello?" he croaked.

"Hello?" a voice answered from the darkness, followed by a blinding light.

Earlier in his ordeal Billy would have been overcome with joy, but now, he attributed it, to him losing his mind, or worse that he had died and he was trying to stay away, from going into the light. He shielded his eyes from the blinding light with his one good hand and closed his eyes for good measure. The light persisted and he heard the faint sound of footsteps in the leaves.

"Billy?" he heard, from the darkness. "Oh, let me turn this light down so I don't blind you," he said.

Billy removed his hand from in front of his face and looked in the direction of the voice. The man pointed the light at the ground beside Billy, making it easier for him to see. He couldn't believe that someone was here. All the hours that he had spent, hoping for someone to rescue him, and here he was, standing before him.

Billy was overcome with emotion and he wept. Then his mind cleared like a lightning bolt had pierced his foggy mind and he realized what the man had said.

"Wait. How did you know my name?" Billy whispered, with great difficulty.

CHAPTER TWENTY-FIVE

Billy was exhausted. He felt as though he had just gone twelve rounds with a prize fighter. In a way, he had, but the prize was Billy's sanity and for the time being, he had won the right to keep it.

He pulled himself from his seated position and stood leaning against the tree. The old man that had been sitting on the bench, had gotten up and was walking toward him. Billy's first thought, was that he was going to visit with someone else, but there was only him and the old man, on the entire lawn. What's this old guy want? I have enough problems without dealing with some Alzheimer patient, Billy thought.

He continued his slow but steady walk toward him. Billy considered walking to a different place, to avoid him altogether, but he stayed despite his better judgement.

The old man was wearing a navy-blue fedora and had a matching handkerchief tucked into his chest pocket. He had a white beard and teeth that were as white as snow. His fiercely blue eyes peered at Billy from behind gold rim glasses. He was wearing blue jean coveralls, like the ones that Jacob used to wear.

"I hope you don't mind me saying son, you look like a person who could use a friend," he said, when he got close enough.

"I don't mean to be rude, but what I need is some quiet time to think," Billy said.

"Is it time you need, or time to get right with God? I don't mean to be pushy, but I've been on this earth longer than you could know and I've seen many things and met many people. Do you know what they all have in common?" the old man asked.

"No, I'm sure I don't," Billy answered, curtly.

The old man either didn't notice Billy's impatience with him or he was unaffected by it. He continued smiling, and pressed on with what he was saying.

"They all have a relationship with God. Some have a good relationship with Him and some have a bad relationship with Him, but they have one nevertheless. I would say that you are on the outs with God. Would that be a fair assumption?" he asked.

Billy wasn't sure why he was even engaging in conversation with this old coot but he couldn't help himself. His smile was so warm and inviting, that it made him feel at ease somehow.

"Yes. I would say that that is a fair assumption. What kind of God would kill my brother and kill my little baby? That's not someone that I care to have a relationship with," Billy retorted.

"You seem angry. I can understand that. Maybe we can talk some other time, when you're not so upset. When you're ready to talk, I'll listen," the old man said.

"Okay," Billy said, rolling his eyes and walked toward the emergency room doors. He had been gone long enough and he needed to get back before Lisa woke up. Besides the old man was crazy, after all.

"If you ever just want to talk, call me. Even if its in the middle of the night, I'll come," he called after Billy.

"Yeah, okay, I'll do that," Billy said, just to humour him, and continued walking.

The old man did serve a purpose. At least he forgot about his troubles for a short time, although he was no closer now to coming up with an idea of how to break the news to Lisa, than he had been earlier.

When Billy returned to Lisa's room she was awake. One look at her and Billy could tell, that there was no need for him to break the bad news to her.

"Where were you? The doctor was just here!" she said.

"I was here the whole time. I just went out to get some fresh air and clear my head," he said, defensively.

"Oh, Billy. Did the doctor talk to you?" she asked, before she broke down and started to cry.

"Yes, he talked to me while you were sleeping," Billy said, sitting down on the bed beside her and hugging her.

"I can't believe this is happening. What are we going to do?" she said, still crying.

"We have each other and we have to believe, that the other baby will be okay."

"You heard what the doctor said. He said that the baby has less of a chance of making it, because he or she was an identical twin. I can't stop thinking about that poor little baby inside of me, that is dead now. We were so happy. Why did this have to happen?"

Billy didn't have any answers. There was nothing that he could say, to comfort her. He just continued to hold her, and then finally said: "As long as we have each other, we can overcome anything."

"But can we Billy? How do we continue on? It feels like my heart and my stomach have been ripped from my body," Lisa said.

"We need to give it time. Time heals all wounds, and we have to hang on to the hope that our baby will make it," Billy said.

"Don't give me that bullshit cliché, that time heals all wounds. I'm hoping like hell that our baby makes it, because I don't know what I will do if he or she doesn't. No matter what, I will think about that poor little dead baby, until my last breath. How can I ever forget about that?" she said, crying uncontrollably again.

Billy didn't answer her. He just held her and rubbed her back, trying to comfort her. He was sad and hurting too, but he understood that it was worse for her. He just needed to be as kind and understanding as he could be right now. He could be her punching bag if that's what she needed. He would do whatever he could for her.

Billy continued holding her until she shrugged her shoulders and tried pulling away from him.

"I just need to be left alone for a while, Billy," she said.

"Okay. I'll just be in that chair over there, if you need anything," he said, pointing to the chair in the corner of the room.

Minutes later Lisa was fast asleep. The combination of losing a lot of blood and the overwhelming emotional stress, had taken its toll. She began muttering in her sleep shortly after and Billy knew that it was her mind trying to make sense of what had happened. Billy was drained as well but he wasn't sure that he would be able to sleep. He was content to just sit and watch her. He knew that in the coming months that she would have many sleepless nights and it was good to see her sleeping peacefully now.

He started to think about the events of the day. Like many of the things in his life, he wished that he could have a second chance to do things differently. He almost lost the love of his life, but he didn't. He was very sad that they lost one of the babies and that the life of the other hung in the balance, but he knew that he would be able to make it through that. Losing Lisa however, would be unbearable. That was something that he wasn't sure he could make it through. He now understood, what his Father must have felt like, when his Mom died.

Billy spent most of the next few days at the hospital, trying to lend support to Lisa. At times, she was receptive to him trying to console her and at times she just wanted to be left alone. Billy tried to remain supportive and followed Lisa's lead, as to what her needs were.

He wished that she would turn toward him instead of turning away, but everyone grieves differently. Hadn't Lisa told him that herself on their first date? There was something else though. He had an unsettling feeling that Lisa blamed him. If he hadn't been so stubborn and would have gotten some help, then none of this would have happened. Billy thought, that if Lisa would have stayed in the house, like he urged her to do, then none of this would have happened. He didn't dare to say that to Lisa, however. Some things were better left unsaid.

Lisa was in the hospital for three weeks and Billy spent every day there, and some nights as well. When it was time for her to go home, it wasn't a joyous occasion at all. Three days prior to her being released, she lost the other baby.

"How do we pick up the pieces and carry on?" Lisa said.

"I don't know. I do know, that I love you and that I will do whatever it takes," Billy said.

"If you hadn't been so stubborn, then none of this would have happened," Lisa said, and then covered her mouth with her hands. "I'm sorry, Billy. I didn't mean it."

"It's okay," Billy said quietly. The problem was, that she did mean it. On some level, she blamed him, and he blamed himself as well.

Now, going home was a very sad event and extremely awkward as well.

Billy and Lisa could always talk about everything and now they could barely look at each other. There was nothing that could be said that would make it okay. Each of them harboured a little resentment and blame toward the other, for the death of their babies.

"Can I get you anything?" Billy asked her. She was curled up in a blanket, looking out the window toward the pond. She never responded. He went over to her and rubbed her on the shoulder. She pulled away from him and he walked dejectedly toward the door and out to the barn.

He wished he could go out onto the stoop and talk to Jacob; he would know exactly what to say.

Billy tried to make her feel loved and tried to comfort her but she wasn't ready. It had been three weeks since she left the hospital and things weren't getting any easier. He hoped that some day soon, she could see again how much he loved her and that she could begin to live again.

In the meantime, Billy had his own heartache to deal with. He had changed a lot in the last few years. The bully, that terrorized children when he was in high school, was long gone. He was now a mature, kind person that would never hurt anyone. That was of course, when he was in control.

CHAPTER TWENTY-SIX

Billy had struggled since that first day at the hospital, to keep the hollowness at bay. It wore him down slowly. Day by day, it continued to eat away at him. It took little pieces of him and wouldn't give them back.

The tell-tale signs began to return. Dark circles formed under his eyes, once again. He stopped shaving, stopped showering and he was in an irritable mood, most of the time now.

Lisa didn't see it at first, but after a while, she couldn't help but notice that there was something going on with Billy.

"Billy. I know that I haven't been there for you lately. Hell, I've been just trying to survive. We can't give up! We can make it through anything, as long as we have each other. Didn't you say that to me, just a few weeks ago?" she said, paused, and then added. "I love you Billy."

Billy couldn't hear the kindness in her voice, he was too far gone.

"Leave me alone. You grieve the way you need to and I'll grieve the way I need to!" he yelled at her.

Lisa looked as though he had slapped her across the face, but he felt no remorse.

"Billy! We're in this together. We have our whole lives ahead of us."

"What do you want me to say? That I'm sorry. Well I am… I'm sorry that I was ever born."

"Don't say that! I'm glad that you were and that I met you. We'll be happy again, just give it some time."

"You don't understand. It's back. I thought it was gone forever, but it's never gone. It's a virus or a demon, I don't know what it is, but it always returns."

"You're not making sense. What are you talking about?"

"I can't fight it any more. I have to get rid of it forever, or we'll never be happy."

Lisa walked over to him and tried to hug him. He pulled away and raised his hand as if to strike her. She recoiled in horror. He lowered his hand and ran for the door.

"Billy! Don't go! Whatever it is, we can figure it out!"

He ran from the house, jumped in his truck and floored it. Gravel went spitting out from beneath the back tires and peppered the stoop and front windows of the old farmhouse. In his rear-view mirror, he saw Lisa standing there, sheltering her face from the flying gravel. She was calling after him, but he didn't care. Billy drove like a madman. He had no destination in mind and never questioned why he was so angry; he just knew that he was. His mind was no longer his own. He was like a co-pilot watching, as his body did things that were foreign to him.

He drove to the coast and stopped at the base of the mountain where several trails converged in one large rest area. His plan was to go up in to the mountains as far away from civilization as possible, until he could regain control of his mind and body. The only way to get rid of it, was to feed it, but this time he meant to starve it. He was going to fight it and this time he expected to win.

Two days ago, he had planned on taking this trip, before he did something he would regret, but he thought, that with Lisa's help he could fight it. Now, he knew that this was something he needed to do on his own, before he hurt Lisa or someone else. He grabbed the back pack that had been sitting in his truck since then. He had packed enough to last him two days. He figured he could starve it out, in that amount of time.

He locked up the truck and threw the keys in the front pocket of his back pack, flung it over his shoulders and began his ascent up the mountain.

The weather was supposed to turn cold later, but he didn't mind. He had a good sleeping bag rolled up under his back pack, so he was prepared. The hike up the mountain should have been a nice diversion for him. The smell of evergreen was all around. The sounds of birds, chipmunks and squirrels, filled the forest. Every once in a while, the trees would give way to spectacular views.

He didn't smell, hear or see anything. He was focused on getting up the mountain and he didn't notice the beauty around him. He walked with his head down, looking at his boots rising and falling on the dirt path.

It had been two hours since he stormed out of the house for no reason and he should have been calmed down by now, but he was still mad as Hell. The circles under his eyes were darker still and the sparkle in his eyes was gone. Now his eyes were dull, lifeless. He smelled of sweat and body odour and his hair was disheveled and his breath was foul.

He had started to climb the mountain with hopes of regaining control of his life. Those thoughts were forgotten miles back and several hundred feet below.

Now, all he could think of was feeding it. If he fed it, it would let him go. If he fed it, it would repay him with an unbelievable euphoria. He had been so sad since the death of his babies. He deserved to feel joy. He deserved to have the pain removed from him and the unbearable weight lifted from his back. It deserved to be fed as well. It was patient. It had waited long enough.

He continued his ascent up the mountain at a torrid pace. He was sweating profusely and he was panting wildly, but he hardly noticed. He just wanted to get as far up the mountain as possible and as quickly as possible. He couldn't remember why; he just knew that it seemed important.

Eventually he had to stop to take a rest. From this vantage point, nearly half- way up the mountain; the valley lay far below and the thin ribbon of road wound its way through the middle.

The cool breeze dried the sweat from his face and he inhaled deeply, the smell of evergreen.

There was the briefest flicker of humanity behind those dull eyes and then the hollowness resumed control once again.

He heard the far-off sound of someone whistling on a trail below him. He removed his back pack, unzipped the large pocket on the front and took out his hatchet. He looked at it lovingly. He ran his thumb down the length of its blade. The sunlight caught the sharp edge and sent light flickering off the trees in front of him. He turned it over in his hand and grabbed it by the handle. He lifted and brought it down in a chopping motion, feeling the weight of it. He smiled for the first time in weeks.

He waited patiently, as the sound of whistling came closer and closer. He was no longer looking down the mountain to catch a peak of the person to whom the whistling belonged. He was now looking down the same trail that he was sitting beside.

He could see the top of someone's head, just cresting the knoll to his right. In a moment, he would see who it was, that had been whistling to him.

There she was, walking slowly toward him. She stopped whistling when she saw him sitting there against a tree. She was a beautiful, petite girl, in her early twenties. She had her brown hair tied back in a pony tail and it flung from side to side when she walked. She was wearing black tights, that did little to hide her muscular legs, and she was wearing an orange tank top with a black, long sleeve shirt tied at her waist. She nodded at him from a distance and he smiled back at her. He got to his feet as she approached. His heart started to race.

"Nice day for a hike," he said, smiling; trying not to show his excitement.

"Sure is. I come here every week," she said.

"I had to take a break, not used to hiking this far," he said, still smiling.

"Hi, my name's Eleanor, but people usually call me Elle," she said, holding out her hand.

He switched the hatchet from his right hand to his left and held out his hand and shook hers.

"Hi, my name is…" he said, pausing, straining to think. "Billy, his name is Billy." he said after an awkwardly long time.

"His name?" she said, laughing uneasily.

"Sorry, I'm really tired and hungry," it said.

"Did you bring a snack? I may have an extra energy bar in my bag," she said, and removed her bag from her back and began rifling through it.

"No, it's okay. I have this," it said, holding up the hatchet.

"What are you going to do with that?" she said smiling, then the smile started to fade, and a look of fear replaced it.

"I'm sorry, I don't mean to scare you."

Elle saw his eyes flicker for a moment. If she were to be asked later, she would have sworn that his eyes had changed from brown to blue and then back again.

"I'm meeting my friends that are just up the trail a little, so I have to get going," she said nervously, turning to walk away.

"But I need to feed. I told you I'm hungry," it said and grabbed her from behind.

"Take what you want! You can have everything! Take it! It's yours!" she pleaded, starting to cry.

He tightened his grip around her neck until she could hardly breathe, leaned in real close until the tip of his nose was touching the inside of her ear. He inhaled deeply, exhaled loudly and inhaled deeply once again.

"I love that smell. I've missed it so much. Can you smell it? The smell of fear," he whispered in her ear, as if he were cuddling with a lover.

Elle squirmed, trying to get away. He tightened his choke hold around her neck once again, until she started to make little gurgling noises. She reached up with her hands and tried to pull his arm away, so that she could breathe. He loosened his grip and let her fall to the ground. She coughed a couple of times, took a deep breath and then tried to get to her feet. He kicked her hard in the ribs with his boot and laughed with delight. It sounded like green twigs breaking on a tree branch, as her ribs gave way. She rolled on to her back, screaming in agony. The contents of her backpack went spraying onto the ground in front of her. He kicked at a couple of the containers, as he stepped closer to where she lay on the ground, in front of him.

He knelt beside her and his knee landed in a large puddle of strawberry yogurt. He flung the container wildly into the bushes and removed the yogurt on his pants with his hand, then wiped it off, with the shirt tied around her waist. He leaned forward and looked into her eyes. He could see the terror. He threw back his head and let out a bone-chilling laugh, that sent a couple of doves perched nearby, flying to safety.

He got up quickly, grabbed some duct tape from his back pack and returned, to kneel beside her.

"Please, please don't!" she begged, sobbing.

"But, I have to," it said.

"You don't have to! Just let me go. You've had your fun, now you can let me go. Please!" she begged, grabbing at his shirt.

There it was again! His eyes flickered from brown to blue and back again.

"Shut up bitch!" it said, and slapped her hard, across the face.

He ripped off a piece of duct tape and placed it across her mouth. He flipped her on to her stomach and held her down with his knee. She tried to scream out from the fresh stab of pain in her ribs but the duct tape muffled her cry. He pulled her arms behind her and wrapped her wrists tightly with the duct tape. He got to his feet, jerked her up to hers and then dragged her over to a tree and pushed her down hard, at the base of it.

He stood back and looked at her, admiring his handiwork. She had large black rings around her eyes and down her cheeks from her mascara. There were blotches of red on her cheeks and her hair was covered in leaves and dirt. But the most delicious part of the whole picture was the terrified look on her face. It was wonderful. He lifted his arms above his head and breathed deeply. He could feel the rush of energy filling him, and it was good. He stayed that way for a minute or two and then went to sit down beside her. The dark circles beneath his eyes were already beginning to fade, and he felt on top of the world.

"You're probably wondering what I'm going to do with you. Well, my dear, that is a very good question and I'm glad you asked. I'm not completely sure, you know? I haven't really thought that far ahead, just kind of living in the moment. Enjoying it, you know?" it said, lovingly.

She tried to say something but it was inaudible because of the duct tape.

"Now, don't waste your energy. You're going to need your strength. You have a very long night ahead of you my dear."

She screamed a loud muffled scream and thrashed wildly, trying to get to her feet, but that only served to delight him even more. He laughed, and grabbed her wrist and held it tight, so much, that she let out a little yelp from the pain. She slumped back down against the tree, letting out a long sigh.

Billy leaned in real close and whispered in her ear, as if he didn't want anyone to hear, but her.

"I'm sorry. I'm so sorry," Billy said.

She turned to look at him, and there was the tiniest flicker of movement in his eyes again.

"What the fuck are you looking at. Just close your eyes and sit there. I'm going over to that tree to rest, and don't get any bright ideas, because I'll be watching you," it said, pointing at a tree across from her.

He sat down hard against the base of the tree. He was exhausted from his hike up the mountain and just needed to rest for a few minutes to figure out what his next plan was. Even though he was tired, he felt great. Everything smelled better, looked sharper. He had filled up a little, but there was still a little more work to be done.

He lay his head back against the rough bark of the tree. It jabbed into the back of his head so he re-positioned himself a couple of times until he was comfortable. He sighed heavily, smiled contentedly and before he knew it, he was fast asleep.

· · · · ·

He was in a large cave. The roof was nearly fifty feet high and the size of a football field. The walls were smooth and dripping with water. The ceiling was mostly bare but a few stalactites hung in the centre. He turned to look in all directions but it looked the same from every angle. No exit or entrance was visible, and the roof was solid rock. Strangely enough, there was plenty of light to see. He walked the circumference of the room looking for a way out, but found none.

Half the room was bare rock and the other half had a few inches of water covering the floor. He was very thirsty and he intended on getting a drink of the inviting water. He walked to the edge and looked down. What he saw shocked him and he jumped back. A gasp escaped him and the sound echoed off the walls. The sound seemed to be taunting him, laughing at him. He stepped forward and peered into the pool of water once again. His Dad's face was looking back at him. It was Billy's reflection but somehow it was his Dad's. He reached up to scratch his head, and the reflection that was his Dad's did the same. He laughed a nervous laugh and his Dad laughed right along with him. The sound of his laugh echoed off the walls of the cave once again. Except this time, he thought that he could hear his name being called as well. He shook his head slightly and then put his fingers in his ears and pulled them out quickly, attempting to pop them. When he had finished, the sound was gone.

He looked back into the pool of water and his Dad was still staring back at him. He had a warm genuine smile on his face.

"Remember what I said Billy. I too had the hollowness visit me, and I defeated it, only when I reconciled with God. You're a good boy, son. Sometimes good people do bad things. Besides, it's not your fault. You can't fight it, it's too strong, it wants to live more than you can know," Bill said.

"I don't want to do the things that it makes me do. It's just too strong," Billy said, clasping his hands to his mouth.

The voice that came out of his mouth was not his. It was the squeaky, scared voice of a nine- year old Billy Johnson.

He went to speak again and found that his voice had returned to normal.

"I'm not sure I can fight it!" Billy said.

"You can't Billy! You can't fight it alone. You need to ask God to help you. He will Billy, all you have to do is ask."

"I've said some real nasty things to Him. I'm not so sure he'll want to help me," Billy said, wiping tears from his eyes.

He looked into the pool at his Dad's reflection. It flickered and then it was him again. It flickered again, but this time it was his reflection looking at him still, but it wasn't. What was looking at him, now had brown eyes instead of blue, and they were dark sightless eyes, without emotion, and he knew what it was. Billy had to look away.

The silence of the cave was broken by the sound of footsteps behind him. He turned around quickly to see an old man in coveralls gingerly making his way across the rocks, strewn about the cave floor.

"Hey!" Billy yelled.

The man looked up briefly, showing his teeth and his white beard, that were both white as snow. He tipped his blue fedora in his direction and then continued on his way.

Billy ran to intercept him but he disappeared behind an outcropping before he could get there. He looked in all directions but there was no sign of him. Billy listened for the sound of footsteps but he heard none. He had just vanished.

Billy sat down on a large rock to think. He put his head in his hands.

I'm sorry for what I've done and I'm sorry for blaming you. I'll try harder, but I need your help, Billy thought.

He awoke with a start. He felt refreshed from his nap, even though it was one of the strangest dreams he had ever had. Most importantly, he felt like himself. He was relieved, but then he remembered Elle.

He looked at the tree across from him, but she was gone. He walked out to the path and looked down it in both directions. She was nowhere to be seen. He went back and grabbed his back pack. He picked up the hatchet, looked at it with disgust and threw it as far into the woods as he could.

He flung the back pack onto his shoulder and walked out to the trail. A muffled scream came from his left and he ran in its direction.

When he rounded the corner, he saw Elle standing on the path. A Grizzly bear cub was behind her and the mother was in front of her. Elle turned her head and saw Billy. A muffled cry escaped her.

"It's okay. I'm okay now," Billy said.

Like she would believe that, he thought.

Billy paused for a moment to assess the situation. There was no way of him getting to Elle without passing the cub and he didn't want to get any closer to it for fear of mom thinking he was going to hurt it.

He stood his ground. Hoping that the cub would move off and take mom with it.

Mom started walking slowly toward Elle and with every step she took forward, Elle took a step backward.

The cub was still standing in the same spot watching Billy. Every step Elle took backward was another step closer to the cub.

Billy could only see brown fur sticking out on either side of Elle. She was blocking his view, so he couldn't see what Mom was doing, but he knew she was close.

Elle took a couple of quick steps back and that was enough for mom. Billy saw her head above Elle's as she stood on her hind legs. Elle screamed and turned to run.

"No!" Billy yelled, but it was too late.

Mom was on top of her before she had made it four feet. Elle turned to look at Billy as if to say, help and then she was gone. Mom swiped at her with one mighty paw and her nails dug deep furrows across her midsection.

Billy thought briefly about the hatchet that he had thrown into the woods and then dismissed it. He thought about standing his ground, but Mom turned to face him, let out a huge roar and then started to run at him. Billy turned and ran across the trail and headed for the cliff.

He looked down and decided it was too far of a drop, so he turned to run down the edge of it, to find a spot that was lower. Mom got to him just as he was turning around.

He put his hands up to shield himself as she came forward. His right hand went right into her mouth and she bit down hard. Searing pain ripped through his hand and he screamed out in agony. She reared up on her back legs and brought her right paw forward. Billy had a split second to recall what Elle had looked like after those huge claws had swiped at her and then he was hurtling through the air to the ground far below.

He flipped end over end and came down hard on his right leg. He could hear it snap from the impact and his head smacked hard against a rock. Blood sprayed from his head and nose. The world swam in front of him and he lost consciousness.

He opened his eyes and at first he was a little dis-oriented. The pain from his hand, leg, ribs and head reminded him, of what had taken place. He was sure, that along with his broken leg, he had broken a couple of ribs as well and may have a collapsed lung to boot. It was painful, just to breath but that might have been, just his ribs. He tried to lift his head, but his neck was stiff and he had a splitting headache. He surveyed the landscape trying to figure out where he was. He was a long way from any trail, but he knew that if he had any hope of being saved, he would have to try getting closer to one.

First order of business, was to try and stop the bleeding in his hand and head. His back pack had gone flying further down the mountain and was of no use to him. He tore two long strips of fabric from his under shirt. He used one to wrap around his hand and the other to wrap around his head. Neither of them stopped the blood flow completely, but it helped. He lifted his arm up to look at his watch and found that it was smashed and rendered useless. He tore it from his wrist and threw it down the mountain. His ribs and head protested at the sudden movement and he lay on his back, panting, trying to overcome the pain.

Billy decided to try crawling out into the open more, in hopes of finding a trail. He knew that the longer he waited, the harder it would be to move. He started crawling but after only fifty feet, he couldn't go any further. He remembered how he could hear Elle whistling from a long way off and it gave him hope. He could call out to anyone passing by, and surely they would hear him, and he would be saved.

He thought about what happened to poor Elle. If he had been stronger, than she would still be alive. Henry would still be alive for that matter. He could still see the scared, desperate expression on her face, when the bear attacked her. Billy closed his eyes to escape the sight of it, but it was still there. That sight was burned into his brain. His to keep, until the day that he died.

CHAPTER TWENTY-SEVEN

The man holding the flashlight didn't answer him. Instead he turned the flashlight toward Billy's battered body, so that he could survey the damage.

"You really did a number on yourself, didn't you?" he asked, instead.

"I guess so. Listen, It really hurts to talk so could you please go get help," Billy struggled to say.

"But I am here to help. Wasn't that you calling for help a few moments ago? You called and I came. That's how it works. Here, have some water," he said, handing Billy a cup.

Billy grabbed at it eagerly with his good hand. He tipped the water toward his mouth and the ice- cold liquid ran down his throat. It was like heaven.

"How was that water so cold?" he asked, now that he could speak easier.

The man didn't answer him. He just kept shining the light toward Billy.

"Thank you for the water. It was amazing, but I've been lying here for a long time and I'm afraid that I'm running out of time. So, anything that you could do to help, would be greatly appreciated," Billy said, sounding a little annoyed.

The initial adrenaline surge and the refreshing water's effects were already wearing off and Billy could feel himself faltering again. He knew that time was of the essence.

"Is it more time you need, or time to get right with God," the man asked.

Billy's heart beat faster. He had heard that before. Where? Why did that seem so familiar? Billy's mind was foggy from days without food or water. He had lost a lot of blood and he was on death's doorstep.

The man didn't wait for an answer he just pressed on.

"That's terrible what happened to poor Eleanor, don't you think?" he asked.

Billy's foggy mind was racing. He was unsure, if this was real or a dream. He had finally lost it and was talking to a bush, or perhaps he was dead and he was being judged.

"I would gladly give my life, if it would bring her back! I would gladly give my life, if it would bring my kid brother Henry back!" Billy yelled at the bush or the man or the night.

He didn't care who he was talking to. The fact remained the same. He was sorry for what he had done and he was sorry for the suffering that he had caused. He had lifted himself up on his elbows and now he fell back to the ground, exhausted from his outburst.

He lay there for a minute collecting himself and then started to speak again, only quieter this time.

"I would never have done those things. It was so strong and I was weak," Billy said, crying.

"Why didn't you ask for help?" the man asked.

"I couldn't ask for help. I though that it was me. I thought that there was something wrong with me. I didn't think anyone could help me," Billy said.

"But, it wasn't you. Let me ask you a question. Was your Dad strong enough to fight it on his own? I'll answer that one for you, because that's an easy one. No, he wasn't strong enough on his own," the man said.

"How do you know about my Dad?" Billy asked.

"Because, I know everything about you Billy. I've always been there. I've just been waiting for you to ask for help. I once told you that if you needed my help, just call, even if it was in the middle of the night. Do you remember that Billy? the man asked.

Billy thought back. Yes, it did seem familiar, just like his voice.

"You're the man that I met at the hospital, the day that Lisa almost drowned! Why are you here? I don't understand," Billy asked.

"I was also there when you brother died but you pushed me away. I was there in the cave just before Eleanor was killed. Do you remember? You apologized, and I am here to accept your apology, my son."

It took all the energy he had left, but Billy propped himself up on his elbows once again. He wanted to get a better look at the man standing in front of him. He was positive that he knew who that would be, but he needed to see it for himself.

The man rotated the flashlight toward himself. The light passed over his jean coveralls and his handkerchief, stuffed easily in his breast pocket. It continued to swing upward until it shone on his snow- white beard, brilliant white teeth, and finally his bright blue fedora.

"So, I'll ask you again. Is it more time that you need, or time to get right with God?" the man asked.

"I figure I'm just about out of time and I'm okay with that. I would say, it's about time, I get right with God," Billy said.

"I would say, you already have," the man said, as Billy Johnson lay back, looked up at the stars, smiled, took his last breath and let it out slowly.

CHAPTER TWENTY-EIGHT

Billy and Henry were waiting on the bridge in the woods. Henry protested being there. Billy wanted to terrorize some of the younger kids on their way to school. Henry was always a softie. He didn't like hurting anyone or bullying them and he pleaded with Billy to stop. Billy wasn't in the mood to listen to Henry try and ruin his fun. Terrorizing kids filled him up almost as much as hurting them, at least in the beginning. It was like a drug and like many drugs however, it became harder and harder for him to get the same satisfaction. Henry became increasingly critical of Billy's actions and he became more vocal about it as time passed. Billy became weary of Henry's constant protestations and he had nearly enough of it.

"Here comes that fat kid, Jack, I think his name is. He should be a good one. He's always fun to pick on; he gets all blubbery and scared. Just follow my lead Henry," Billy said.

"Okay," Henry said, staring at the ground.

Billy knew that Henry didn't like picking on people and he'd had enough of it, but he didn't care.

"Oh look! He has a nice, shiny, Scooby -Doo lunch box and a new hat by the look of it. Should be easy to get him going," Billy said.

"Hey fatty!" Billy called out.

Jack continued to trudge along. Billy wasn't sure if he didn't hear him, or if he was ignoring him. He felt the anger rising in him, something that had been happening more and more frequently. His desire to feel the rush of other people's emotions drove him more than anything, and anyone that stood in his way felt his wrath.

"Hey fatty, I'm talking to you," Billy called to him, from his perch atop the railing.

Jack kept trudging along toward the bridge.

"Are you hard of hearing or just stupid?" Billy yelled at him.

"I don't want any trouble. I just want to get to school," he said, meekly.

"No problem, but if you want to cross the bridge, you'll have to pay the toll," Billy said.

"I don't have any money," he said and kept walking.

He was nearly at the bridge now and Billy jumped down from the railing to block his way.

"If you want to pass you'll have to give Henry there a blowjob," Billy said, motioning toward his brother.

"Leave him alone, Billy," Henry pleaded.

Billy spun to look at Henry, ready to tear a strip off him. Henry had an agonized look on his face and Billy's mood softened. There was something familiar about the look on his face. Billy had raised his fist, ready to punch Henry square in the nose, but he lowered his arm. He stood staring off into space, and Jack took that as his cue to get across the bridge, as fast as he could.

Billy stood for a full two minutes staring into nothing.

"Come on Billy! Stop fooling around! You're scaring me!" Henry begged, but Billy didn't move or even blink.

Billy remembered holding Henry for hours, while he waited for help at the bottom of the quarry. He remembered meeting Jacob and Lisa. In fact, he remembered everything. A huge smile spread across Billy's face and he started laughing. He reached out and grabbed hold of his kid brother and hugged him hard and wouldn't let go. He was crying and laughing at the same time, but he wouldn't let go of Henry.

"Come on Billy. You're hurting me. What's wrong with you?" Henry protested.

Billy finally let go of Henry and held him at arm's length. Tears were streaming down his face and he was smiling from ear to ear.

Billy could see it on his face. Henry thought that his big brother had finally lost his marbles.

"I love you Henry. You know that, right?" Billy said.

"Fuck you, Billy. There's something wrong with you," Henry said, laughing uneasily.

"Not any more, little brother. Not any more. Come on I'll buy you an ice cream cone and then we have somewhere that we need to be," Billy said.

"What about school?"

"It'll be there tomorrow. We have to take care of this today. We have to set it right," Billy said.

Billy walked with Henry to get an ice cream and he never stopped smiling the entire way. He couldn't believe it was happening and he didn't know how. All he knew, was that he was the happiest he'd ever been in his entire life, and this time, he was going to get it right.

"So where are we going after we get ice cream?" Henry asked.

"Just live in the moment Henry. Enjoy your ice cream and then we'll talk about it," Billy said.

Henry ate his ice cream greedily and it was gone before he knew it.

"Did you even taste it?" Billy asked, then bought him another one.

"Come on. You can eat it while we walk."

"Where are we going, Billy?"

"We are going to spend the day with Dad. He's not a bad guy, he's just had bad things happen to him," Billy said.

When they got back to the house, their Dad was still in bed. He was hung over, from another late night at the bar. Billy though it was best not to wake him, so he and Henry went downstairs and played a couple of board games until he was up and about.

"Hey Henry, let me do the talking when we talk to Dad. I have to try and figure a way to reach him, without him getting pissed and throttling me. In case I can't, I don't want you getting hurt. Okay?"

"No problem, Billy. I don't want to be on the wrong end of his bad mood," Henry said.

They finished their game and they could hear their Father moving around upstairs.

"Okay. Here goes," Billy said.

"Good luck. You'll need it," Henry said, drawing his finger across his throat.

Billy went up the stairs and found his Father sitting on the couch, with an opened beer sitting on the table in front of him.

"What are you doing home? Shouldn't you be in school?" he asked.

"We were walking to school but something happened on the way, and I figured that I needed to talk to you about it, right away," Billy said.

"What's so important that it couldn't have waited until after school? Can't you see that I'm busy," he said, picking up his beer and taking a swig.

"I think it's very important. Remember when you promised Henry and I that you were going to be a better Father? You did really well for a while and then you kind of fell off a bit. Well, a lot actually," Billy said.

Billy looked over to where Henry was sitting at the top of the stairs. Henry was listening, and he cringed at what he said.

"Well you little shit!" Bill said.

"Hold on Dad! I didn't come in here to insult you. You'll understand a little more in a minute," Billy said.

"Henry, go back downstairs until we're through," Billy yelled.

He heard the sound of hurried footsteps, descending the stairs to the basement.

"I'm not blaming you Dad. I understand. It's not your fault," Billy said, reaching out to grab hold of his Dad's hand and deftly moving the beer bottle out of his Dad's reach.

The look on his face softened a little and he looked as if he was more receptive, to what Billy had to say.

"I know it's not your fault. I know it's strong and it's hard to fight. You can't fight it alone and you don't have to. That's the good news, you don't have to. You have me, Henry and God," Billy said.

It looked like he had him hooked until he mentioned God, then his expression hardened once again.

"I don't know what you're talking about!" Bill said, angrily.

"I think you do."

"What's not my fault? That my wife and your Mother died way too early and that God abandoned us. You're right it's not my fault. It's His. It's His fault," he said, crying.

Billy squeezed his Dad's hand and then continued.

"I'm talking about the hollowness. It's not your fault, it's the hollowness,"

Billy said.

Bill looked as if he had just seen a ghost.

"What? How do you know about that? I've never told a soul about it," Bill asked, looking confused.

"You told me about it, in another life," Billy quipped.

"No really? How did you know?" Bill asked, sitting on the edge of his seat now.

"I had a dream. It was the most realistic dream I've ever had. God told me! He told me a lot of things but the big ones were about the hollowness, and that you needed Him to fight it. He said that you couldn't fight it alone, that he has always been there and that you just have to ask for help."

He hoped God would forgive him for a little white lie. He though that under the circumstance, that it was probably okay. It was for a good cause, after all.

"You're right. I need help. I can do better for you kids. I'm sorry Billy," Bill said, grabbing Billy, pulling him close and hugging him hard. Henry ran from the top of the stairs and joined in, hugging his brother and Dad.

"I'm sorry Henry," Bill said.

"It's okay Dad," Henry simply said.

That was early afternoon on a Friday and that Sunday the three Johnson boys got dressed up in their best duds and they attended church together, for the first time in many years.

Billy and Henry entered the church first, followed closely by their Father. Billy led them up the aisle, to an empty pew near the front. He let Henry sit down first and then his Father. He stood for a second and looked around the room. He had that feeling that he was being watched. He looked to his right across the aisle and an older gentleman with bright white teeth and a beard as white as snow, smiled, tipped his blue fedora in his direction and then took it off and set in on the pew beside him. Billy smiled widely in response and gave him a little wave.

"Who's that?" Henry whispered in Billy's ear, when he sat down.

"A good friend. Maybe I'll introduce you two to him, if I get the chance later," Billy said, smiling.

CHAPTER TWENTY-NINE

Years passed and the three Johnson boys, couldn't have been closer. Bill resurrected his failing business and they moved to a nicer house. Billy worked hard to get good grades and he worked in his spare time, to save money to buy a truck. That's when he wasn't spending time with Henry and his Dad.

Billy had to make another thousand dollars and then he would have enough to buy the truck at the used car lot, at the edge of town. He was hoping that it wouldn't be sold in the meantime. He went to visit it a couple times a week, just to make sure that it was still there, and to see if it had dropped in price.

On his seventeenth birthday, he went to visit it on the lot, and was heartbroken to find a sold sign on the windshield.

He rode his bike slowly home, slipped into his bedroom and laid down on his bed.

Henry stuck his head in, a few minutes later.

"We're leaving soon. You'd better get ready, or you're going to be late for your own birthday supper," Henry said.

"What's wrong with you, sour puss?" he asked, when he realized that Billy was moping.

"Nothing! I'll be out in a minute," Billy snapped at him.

"Come on, Billy! We're going to be late," Bill yelled from the kitchen.

"Coming!" Billy yelled back.

They jumped in the car and headed downtown to go to the restaurant.

"I almost forgot. I have to stop by and get something on our way," Bill said, swinging the car around and heading back the other way.

"What do you have to get?" Billy asked.

Henry couldn't contain himself any longer. He was fidgeting and nervously tapping on the headrest of Billy's seat.

"Quit it, Henry! What's wrong with you?" Billy yelled.

"Okay, you two. Settle down," Bill said.

Henry couldn't have planned it any better. Not that he meant to. But it did serve to distract Billy and he wasn't paying attention to where they were headed.

Bill swung the car into the parking lot of the used car dealership and Henry squealed with delight. Billy finally caught on.

"Happy birthday Billy," Bill and Henry said, in unison.

Billy jumped from the car and ran to the truck. His Dad met him there and handed him the keys, while Henry pulled the sold sign from the windshield and threw it in the box of the truck.

"You two want to meet me at the restaurant?" Bill asked.

"What?" Billy asked.

"I took care of everything earlier today. She's legal." Bill said, smiling widely.

"Let's go! What are you waiting for?" Henry said, from the passenger side seat.

Billy walked over to his Dad and wrapped his arms around him and hugged him long and hard.

"I love you Dad. You're the greatest Dad ever!" he said.

"I love you too, son. Now get! I'll meet you at the restaurant."

．　　　．　　　．　　　．　　　．

Billy swung up into the cab of his new truck, and it was like coming home again.

"This is awesome!" Henry cried.

"It sure is. We're a couple of the luckiest guys alive," Billy said.

They went out and celebrated his birthday and they had a great time, but later that night when Billy was alone in his bedroom, he started to feel a little sad. His life was great now, there was no denying it. Henry was still with him and he couldn't begin to explain, how incredible that was. They both had an extremely close relationship with their Dad. Life was good all around, except…

He thought about Lisa everyday and about Jacob and the small town that he had called home for several years. He missed Lisa so much and now that he had the means to do so; he had to go see her. First thing in the morning, he meant to talk to his Dad.

Sleep didn't come easy that night and he dreamt when it did come. He dreamt of the farm and Jacob, but mostly of Lisa. In the morning, he lay awake in bed, waiting for his Dad to get up, listening to the birds chattering outside his window. When he heard him stir, he was right there to talk to him.

"Hey Dad. School's done now. I'd like to go on a bit of a road trip and maybe find some summer work, if that's okay?"

"I think that would be good for you, expand your horizons. Besides, it will give me time, to spend some alone time with Gwen."

"So, Henry's coming with?" Billy said, excitedly.

"That's if you don't mind?" Bill said.

"Of course not, that's awesome. I'm going to tell him right now," Billy said, and ran to find Henry.

.   .   .   .   .

The two of them left two days later and they were both super excited to be going on a road trip. Billy of course was even more excited, that he was going to see the love of his life.

Billy and Henry talked excitedly the entire trip. Several times Billy had to tell Henry to stop yelling at him; he was that excited.

They took their time, stopping when they saw something of interest. Henry had to stop every half hour or so to go pee anyway, he was just that amped up.

As far as Henry knew, they didn't have a destination in mind. They were just two brothers on a road trip and wherever they ended up, they ended up. Billy was definitely enjoying the road trip, but he was anxious to get to his destination.

Finally, Billy pulled into the parking lot of Angel's diner. He turned off the ignition and sat thinking for a minute. What was he going to say? She wouldn't know him from Adam. Then he thought, she didn't know him the first time either, and she had her eye on him, maybe it'll be the same this time.

Henry had gotten out of the truck and was holding the front door open.

"What are you doing space cadet? Are you coming or what? I really need to pee," he said urgently.

"Yeah, coming," Billy said, as he ran for the door.

Henry disappeared into the bathroom and Billy stood at the entrance, surveying the room. He saw Cheryl and Stacy working, but he didn't see Lisa. Maybe she was in the back and she would be out in a minute. He stood waiting to see, before he sat down.

Henry came out of the bathroom and stood beside Billy.

"Are we waiting to be seated or something? I think we can probably just sit anywhere," Henry said.

Billy turned to look at him.

"Henry, you got water on the front of your pants. It looks like you pissed yourself," he whispered.

Henry looked down and saw the dark spot on the front of his pants and covered it quickly with his hand and disappeared, back into the bathroom.

"You can sit anywhere you like, hon," Cheryl said.

"Sure… okay. Is Lisa working today?" Billy asked.

"Sure enough, hon. She's just getting on shift. She'll be out in a jiffy. That means that I can go home. Thank God," she said.

She no sooner finished saying that, and Lisa came out of the back. She was still fixing her apron as she walked. She grabbed a notepad and came over to the booth, where Billy was sitting.

Apparently, the first time he came into this diner he never noticed her. Well, he sure noticed her now. He had a hard time playing it cool. He wanted to grab her, kiss her and make love to her right then and there, but that probably wouldn't go over very well.

Henry wasn't back from the bathroom yet and Billy was glad for it. He was probably using the hand drier to dry the front of his pants. That gave him the opportunity to talk to Lisa, without Henry distracting them.

Billy couldn't take his eyes off her, but Lisa still didn't look up, until she was standing right in front of him.

"Can I take your order? Oh, I didn't even give you a menu yet. I'll be right back," she said.

"It's fine, don't need one," Billy said.

"Oh, okay," Lisa said, looking up for the first time.

She started to smile at him and then she started to blush. Billy took that as a good sign.

He ordered drinks and waited for Henry to return from the bathroom. Agnes and Herbert came in and sat down in the booth beside him and Lisa made her way over to them. She almost took out a table with her knee, not watching where she was going. She was too busy trying to sneak a peak at the handsome stranger in booth number seven and her face turned bright red from embarrassment.

She took their order and then went into the kitchen to get Billy's and Henry's.

"She's hot!" Henry whispered to Billy, when he returned.

"Knock it off! she was talking to me while you were in the bathroom, so don't get any ideas. You're looking at the future Mrs. Billy Johnson. Besides, she's too old for you," Billy said.

"Okay, what ever you say. I'm fifteen; I'm not a little kid anymore," Henry scoffed.

Lisa's eyes never left Billy's as she walked toward their table. She put their order down and then spun to walk away. Her skirt flung out and up and Billy caught a glimpse of her underwear beneath. Apparently, Henry did as well.

"See hot!" Henry said.

Billy punched him hard in the shoulder.

"What did you do that for?" Henry asked.

"I told you. She's in to me. So, just back off," Billy said.

Lisa peeked over her shoulder, and Billy winked at her. She spun back around and walked back to their table.

"Have we met before? I feel like I've seen you two before, but I can't place you," she asked, looking at Billy and ignoring Henry.

"I guess we just have familiar faces. We're just passing through. Hey, we were planning on going out to the coast. I heard about some cliff that you can jump off, into the ocean. Do you know the place?" Billy asked.

"Of course I do. I used to go there with my cousins all the time. I'd still go, but I don't have a way there," she said.

"Well, we're going, if you want to go with us," Billy said.

"I'm working. Besides, you're complete strangers."

"We don't bite, I promise," Billy said.

"Might nibble a bit," Henry said, and Billy shot him a look.

"You guys seem harmless enough. I'm off at five, swing by here and I'll make a call to my cousin Hailey, to see if she wants to come with."

"Sounds good," Billy said.

Lisa left and went back into the kitchen.

"I hope her cousin is as hot as she is," Henry whispered.

"Can you stop calling her hot, please?" Billy said.

"Well she is. What are we going to do in this little town, for three and a half hours?" Henry asked.

"I saw an ad up on the board when we came in, for farm labourers, for the growing season. I thought we could go check it out," Billy said.

They ate their lunch, and Billy's burger was every bit as good, as he remembered them being. He took off in the direction of the farm.

He pulled slowly into the lane way and parked beside the house. He got out and stood looking out over the barnyard and the fields beyond. He couldn't help but notice how much the buildings needed painting. He had spent four weeks painting them the first time. Oh well, he thought, at least this time he had Henry to help him. Then he turned and stood looking at the old farm house. The stoop was directly in front of him and it looked the same as he remembered. Jacob's rocker was still sitting in the same position with the tiny tea table sitting beside it. The ivy that grew all along the sides of the stoop, were still there providing shade on hot summer days. The worn steps from years of climbing them, still looked the same and the white paint on the pillars holding up the roof, were cracked and peeling the same as they had been, the first time that he saw them. He thought about all those nights passing the time, talking to Jacob.

"Are you alright? You've been acting strangely all day," Henry asked.

"Fine," Billy answered.

Jacob had heard the truck pull in and came out onto the stoop. He made his way down the steps and came out to meet them.

"She's a beauty," Jacob said, pointing to Billy's truck.

"Just got her for my birthday, maiden voyage," Billy said, calmly.

He wanted to run to him and hug him for all he was worth. He missed him so much. He couldn't believe that he was standing here in front of him. He gave the eulogy at his funeral, for God's sake. Billy raised his eyes to the heavens and mouthed the word, sorry.

"I always wanted to buy my son a truck for his birthday, but sadly it never happened," Jacob said, sighing.

"What brings two strapping boys like yourselves, all the way out here? Ah, let me guess. You want work for the summer," Jacob said.

"We were hoping," Billy said.

"Well, let's start with introductions. I'm Jacob," he said, holding out his hand.

Henry shook his hand and then Billy did as well. Billy had a hard time letting go.

"Good strong handshake, son," Jacob said to Billy. "You two have names?"

"I'm Billy Johnson and this is my kid brother Henry. Pleased to meet you, Sir," Billy said.

"Well now, you don't hear that expression, kid brother, all that much any more. You seem awful familiar to me. You sure we haven't met before?" Jacob asked.

"Maybe in a previous life or something," Billy said, laughing nervously.

"Yeah maybe. Well, come up onto the stoop and take a load off. I'll fix us some drinks and we can get acquainted. I should warn you though. I've been known to talk a few ears off in my time. I sure hope you boys have some time to kill," he said, pausing.

"That reminds me of another expression. Are you boys religious?" Jacob asked.

"Yes Sir, we are. We never miss Sunday mass," they answered.

"The expression goes something like this. Let me see if I can get this straight. Is it time you need, or time to get right with God? Something like that," he said, winked at Billy, and then went into the house to get their drinks.

THE END

View other Black Rose Writing titles at www.blackrosewriting.com/books and use promo code **PRINT** to receive a **20% discount** when purchasing.

BLACK ROSE writing™

CPSIA information can be obtained
at www.ICGtesting.com
Printed in the USA
LVOW03s0447250418
574746LV00002B/3/P